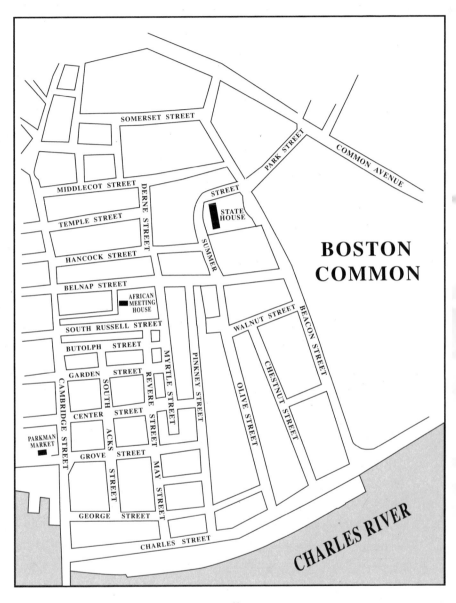

Beacon Hill, Boston
Based on John G. Hales Map - 1814
courtesy, Norman B. Leventhal Collection
Boston Public Library

Beyond Freedom

By

Patricia Q. Wall

FALL ROSE BOOKS
Kittery Point, Maine
www.fallrosebooks.com

This is a work of fiction. Names, characters, places and incidents are either the product of the author's imagination or, if real, are used fictitiously.

BEYOND FREEDOM

Copyright © 2010 Patricia Q. Wall

First Edition

Published by
FALL ROSE BOOKS
P.O.Box 39
Kittery Point, Maine 03905
www.fallrosebooks.com

ISBN: 0-9742185-1-0
Library of Congress control number: 2009935140

1) Afro-American – History 1812 – Juvenile Fiction
2) Afro-American – New England – History 1812 – Juvenile Fiction
3) Afro-American – Boston (MA) – History 1812 – Juvenile Fiction
4) Afro-American – Portsmouth (NH) – History 1730-1806 – Juvenile Fiction

Cover painting by Debby Ronnquist
Design by AD-CETERA GRAPHICS
Printed by J.S. McCarthy Printers, Augusta, ME, U.S.A.

To my dear children, Bradford, Valerie and Lawrence and grandchildren, Henry, Brenna, Calvin, Patti, Mark, and Rhys

To Liz Nelson, kind friend and mentor

Chapter One
Beacon Hill – Boston Massachusetts
Wednesday, 24 June 1812

"Oh, please, don't let them catch me!" Matty tore around the corner of a large brick house and dashed into an alleyway. Not far behind her, came the boys' angry shouts.

"Come here, girl! We'll learn you your place!"

"Negroes don't belong up here!"

Matty rushed on down the alley, only to see what appeared to be a dead end with no place to hide. On all sides, high board fences blocked her view. Suddenly, part way down the alley, she saw a gate opening in the fence and a hand beckoning to her.

"Quick! In here!" called a voice softly.

Gratefully, fifteen-year-old Matty hurried inside and closed the gate. Turning around, she saw a smiling young white girl signaling for silence. Without waiting, the girl grabbed Matty's hand, hurried her across the backyard and down steep steps into a cellar beneath the house.

"You'll be safe here," she whispered. "Those nasty boys won't find you."

Out of breath and heart pounding, Matty simply stared at the other girl as they hunkered down on dusty wooden steps. The girl's well-to-do appearance and fashionable clothes made Matty feel self-conscious. She tugged her mob cap further down and began pushing straggling hair back into the dark curly mass beneath it. Then she smoothed her white apron across a plain grey cotton dress and drew its long skirt closer to hide dusty, worn shoes.

Meanwhile, out in the alley, came more shouting and banging on wooden fences.

"You sure she came this way?" shouted a boy's voice.

"Yeah, she must be hiding behind a fence somewhere," another shouted.

"Don't worry," Matty's companion whispered, "they can't see us here." Leaning closer, she said, "My name's Lydia. What's yours?"

Matty's reply was lost in sudden noise from out in the yard as a deep male voice shouted, "Get away from here, you wicked boys…or I'll get the constable after you."

Curious, the girls peeked up over the cellar opening in time to see a tall, broadly built white man leaning over the back fence and shaking his fist.

"There now," said Lydia in a chirpy sort of voice, "you're safe. That's our butler, George. He won't stand for any foolishness."

Settling back down on the cellar steps, they waited for things to quiet down. Matty glanced at Lydia's appearance again, noting a slightly chubby face and long blond hair drawn up haphazardly by a wide pink ribbon. She's got freckles like I do, Matty thought, but her green eyes look strange. I much prefer my brown ones.

"Now please," Lydia spoke up, "tell me your name

again. And, why were those boys chasing you?"

"I don't know," said Matty, her voice calming now to its usual mellow tone. "I just came up Belknap Street this afternoon to walk out on the Common, to see the trees and the green meadow. It's such a pretty day. Then suddenly, those white boys just came at me. So I ran. They wouldn't let me go back the way I came and I took the wrong street. Now I'm not sure where I am."

"You're at the Bainbridge's house at the upper end of Walnut Street," said Lydia, "just around the corner from Olive Street. We've only lived here about a year," she chattered on, "but Mama thinks we ought to live on Beacon Street. She keeps pestering Papa to have a fancier house built, one that looks out on the Common and ...." Suddenly, Lydia stopped and looked closer at Matty. "Oh, my," she said, "your sleeve is torn."

Embarrassed, Matty clutched at a small tear at the top of her left sleeve. The frightening moment of its tearing flashed through her mind. She had barely escaped that white boy's reach.

"You still didn't tell me your name," said Lydia.

"It's Matty...Matty Warren Smith."

"Well, Matty, I can fix your sleeve good as new," said Lydia popping up. "You just wait here and I'll get my sewing basket."

"That's most kind of you, but there's no need." Matty responded firmly, but politely. "I must get back home now. If you'll just show me a safe way to go, I'll —-"

"Oh, fixing that tear won't take long," interrupted Lydia as she hurried away to another flight of steps further back in the cellar. "And, I'll bring you a nice cool drink of water, too," she called out.

For goodness sake, Matty thought in annoyance. Does she think I don't know how to sew! If only I was sure of a safe way to go, I'd leave right now. Oh well, I better wait and get directions. I'll just decline her sewing offer when she gets back.

Ten minutes later, despite Matty's wishes, Lydia was finishing the last of a dozen small stitches at the top of that sleeve. Though Matty had tried, there had been no easy way to dissuade the girl without being rude.

"There now," said Lydia, "that didn't take long." She leaned in and cut the thread with her teeth, then looked up and grinned. "Mama says doing that's gonna ruin my teeth, but I don't believe it."

During the sewing, Matty had been studying Lydia. I guess I shouldn't be ungrateful to her. She does seem really kind and thoughtful and she has such a wonderful, friendly smile.

Then, unbidden, her grandmother's cautionary words came to mind, "*You've got to be careful around white folks. They might seem friendly, but you can't always count on that.*"

Oh, but that couldn't be true of this girl, Matty silently told herself.

For her part, Lydia also liked what she saw. She had never had such close contact with a black person before and never conversed with one. Fascinated, she glanced at Matty's dark brown face drawn over high cheek bones. Her wide-set eyes above a slightly broad nose and full, soft lips presented a gentle, open expression.

This girl's not at all like what Mama says Negroes are, Lydia thought. She looks clean and neat and she certainly speaks intelligently.

"How old are you?" she asked Matty

"I'm fifteen."

Lydia smiled in delight. "Why, we're the same age, almost. I'll be fifteen on the fourth of July – a great day for me. I always pretend that the whole nation is celebrating *my* birthday."

"Miss, I need to get home now," said Matty as she stood up and began ascending the steps. "If you would please show me a way back to Belknap Street, maybe through another alleyway so those boys wouldn't see me."

"Oh, I can do better than that," said Lydia, following Matty out into the yard. "I'll get George to escort you and see you safely home."

"No, I don't think that would be a good idea," replied Matty. "I don't want my grandmother to know where I've been."

"Well," Lydia persisted, "George can escort you part way, watch you go down Belknap Street, make sure no harm comes to you."

"I guess that would be all right. And I do thank you for all your kindness."

"I'm glad I was here to help," Lydia replied. Smiling at Matty, she suddenly thought, I wish I could get to know more about this interesting girl, maybe have an opportunity to question her — find out more about those Negro people living on the other side of Beacon Hill. And, with that thought came an idea, one she would need to think about. Do a bit of plotting and planning.

"Matty," she said. "If I wanted to get a message to you, how would I find you?"

The question startled Matty. If I'm lucky, she thought, my folks won't find out about today's adventure. But, if this girl sends a message to the house there'd be no way to avoid the truth.

"I don't want to be unkind," Matty said, "but I don't think you should send messages to me."

Lydia simply gave a slow smile. "Well, never mind about that," she said. "I'll go get George to see you safely on your way." Silently, she told herself, I think I might find a way to get what I want.

Chapter Two

$\mathcal{G}$oing down Belknap Street was certainly easier than the coming up had been. Even so, Matty watched her footing on that steepest of Boston's hills. Patches of moss on old cobblestones could easily send the unwary person tumbling out of control. Halfway down, Matty stopped and turned around to look back up hill. In the distance, the butler, George, still kept watch on her safe progress. Waving a thank-you, she turned and proceeded on down to Cambridge Street at the bottom.

The closer she came to that busy street, the more a different world assailed her senses. Leaving the sunny, peaceful and wind-cleansed air at the top of Beacon Hill, Matty descended into a crowded neighborhood known as the North Slope Village. Here, scattered among a population of working-class and poor white people, were more than seven hundred black residents – the largest such group in Boston.

Upon reaching the base of the hill, Matty turned left and carefully made her way home. She only had two and a half blocks to go, but obstacles were numerous, no matter the distance.

Cambridge Street, the main road leading from West Boston Bridge to the heart of the town, was clogged with horse-drawn wagons, carriages and riders on horseback. Dodging among them were men with pushcarts and wheelbarrows. Matty's ears rang from the noise of iron-clad wheels rumbling over cobblestones, the clatter of horseshoes and street vendors' shouting.

At times, when she had to leave the narrow stepping-stone sidewalk to skirt around shopkeepers' stalls, she paid close attention not only to traffic but to avoiding those ever-present patches of horse manure. And always, she stayed alert for any shouts from tenement windows above her head. Though Boston authorities frowned on the practice, some residents still tossed wash water down onto the street.

A sudden gust of wind failed to freshen the hot summer air. Instead, it merely stirred unpleasant odors which had settled in against the steep rise of Beacon Hill. Their components were all too familiar to Matty. In addition to street smells and ever-present wood smoke from a multitude of hearth fires, there came a sour, musty odor from several large breweries and more than thirty rum distilleries north of Cambridge Street. Rancid animal smells drifted in from that area's slaughterhouses and factories which boiled down fat-trimmings for soap-making and candles. But over all that there was a noxious, swampy smell coming from what remained of the old mill pond beside the Charles River. That huge pond was slowly being filled in to make space for new streets. However, its long use as a dumping site for town sewage, dead animals and trash was now creating a new and unpleasant atmosphere for surrounding residents. And, with summer's coming heat, Matty knew matters would surely grow worse.

"It's not fair," she muttered angrily, as she rounded the corner of Butolph Street and headed for their small rented house, the third one on the left. "We shouldn't have to live on this smelly side of the hill."

Entering the narrow hallway of their house, Matty was immediately confronted by her grandmother Bess.

"Where in the world have you been?" the woman demanded as she stood in the doorway of the front room kitchen. "You should have been home long before this!"

"Oh, I only went for a little walk, Gramma." Matty attempted to hurry past the doorway, but Bess stopped her.

"Not so fast," she said, reaching out to take hold of her arm. "I want to know where you were all this time. I sent you to deliver those loaves of bread nearly three hours ago."

Drawing the girl further into the kitchen, Bess let go of Matty's arm and wearily settled her stout, elderly body into a wooden armchair by the front window. She stared up into Matty's eyes with a stern look.

"Where did you take this walk?" she asked. "And mind, I want the truth, as always."

Standing there, Matty struggled with what to say. She couldn't bring herself to tell lies, but maybe she could avoid telling everything.

"Well," she said, heaving a sigh, "after I delivered your loaves of bread to Reverend Mr. Jennings at the meeting house I started to come back home but…well, it was such a pretty day and all, so I thought I'd walk a little further up Belknap hill and see some trees and see what's going on up there and…." Matty burst into tears. "Oh Gramma, I'm awful sorry. I was so frightened and I didn't know where else to go."

"What happened, child? What did you do?"

While dabbing at her face with her apron, Matty poured out the whole story. Her grandmother listened in stony silence.

"What a foolish and dangerous thing to do," Bess finally said. "You know you're not supposed to leave the neighborhood on your own. And certainly, you are never to go up there alone. Not only were you in danger from that gang of white boys, but you might have been arrested by the constable."

"Why would I be arrested, Gramma?"

"Because Africans are not allowed on the Common. There's a law against us being there. I'm sure we must have told you that."

"I don't think you did. Oh please, Gramma, don't tell Papa where I was." Another flood of tears overtook Matty.

"Well, we'll have to see about that," replied Bess. "You go wash your face, then get back here to help me with supper. The men should be home any time now."

As Matty stepped out into the hallway leading to the back door, she heard her grandmother mutter, "Foolish, foolish girl. She's headed for real trouble if we don't watch out."

On the small back porch under a rickety slanted roof, Matty lifted a bucket of water out from under a wash bench and partially filled a tin basin.

Using a bit of homemade soap, she cleansed her face and arms, then tossed the wash water over nearby bushes. While toweling off, she studied her face in a small looking glass hanging on the wall above the bench.

"Africans aren't allowed on the Common," she whispered in a mocking voice. "What a ridiculous idea. That place is meant for everyone. That's what 'common' means. How could they make such a law!"

Fighting her anger, she turned to look out across their tiny, ever so neat back yard. In spite of herself, she smiled. Every inch reflected her great uncle Ned's prideful care.

Though much of the space was taken up by a large wood pile beside the privy, the rest of it contained neat vegetable beds. Here and there against the surrounding wooden fence, young shoots of hollyhocks and morning glories were reaching for sunshine. Just beyond a side gate stood the neighborhood well.

Unlike some residents, Ned refused to allow garbage or refuse to accumulate in the yard. Most evenings, after supper, he carried their slop bucket over to a neighbor who kept several pigs. Other refuse –bones, broken crockery and such – he took to a wharf near the West Boston Bridge. There, as was commonly done, he tossed it into the Charles River.

"Matty," Bess hollered, disrupting the daydreaming, "Stop dawdling and get back in here this minute!"

"I'm coming, Gramma." Matty turned the wash basin upside down on the bench and draped the towel across a wooden peg. "Work, work, work… that's all I ever do around here," she grumbled.

Returning to the front room, Matty found her father Peter, her great uncle Ned (Bess's twin brother) and some of their boarders already seated at the supper table in the middle of the room. Their friendly chatter and aromas of food lifted her spirits somewhat.

"Matty, don't stand around," Bess huffed. "Come turn the mackerel before they burn, then rake those potatoes and onions out of the coals."

Perspiring heavily, sixty-six-year-old Bess turned back to the open fireplace to continue orchestrating supper for eleven people. Such cooking was an exhausting and a dangerous job, one she had been doing all her life. But, from the slowness of her movement and repeated soft huffing, it was clear that age was taking its toll.

In the middle of the large brick recess, a bright log fire licked at several kettles suspended from an iron crane. Below them, off to one side and dangerously close to the front of the hearth, were two piles of hot coals. On one pile sat an iron skillet containing mounds of sizzling and sputtering cornmeal coated fish. In the other pile of coals were buried potatoes and onions. Matty carefully tucked up her long skirts before stepping into the dangerous task.

"And how's our Matty, today?" Ned called out. He was seated at the upper end of the long pine table, his back to the window and the late afternoon sunlight.

Glancing back, Matty smiled at him and at the sun's halo effect around his gleaming bald head with its tuffs of curly white sideburns. "I'm all right, Uncle," she replied fondly before resuming work.

"Well, it sure looks to me like you are." Ned grinned and turned to a younger man sitting on his left. "You know, Peter, your daughter is looking more like her mama every day."

"Yes," said Peter, "it's kinda haunting how much Matty looks like my Matilda. Just wish the poor woman had lived to watch her baby grow up."

"Guess it won't be long 'fore your pretty daughter catches some young fella's eye," said Sam, a heavy-set, middle-aged black man seated to the right of Ned. "My Annie wasn't much older when I first set eyes on her.

Ain't that right, honey?" He put his arm around his young wife next to him, but her pale brown face showed no reaction. Silently, she continued to struggle with two squirm-

ing children beside her, trying to keep the little girls from
crawling up on the table.

Just then, two more boarders, young black men,
entered the room and settled down on the bench next to Sam.
"Good evening, folks," said one. The other man only gave a
half-hearted wave. The contrast in their appearance was striking. The silent one, named Dan, wore shabby, stained clothing
that gave off a strong odor of tar, a constant reminder of his
work as an oiler in a rope factory. He seemed unconcerned by
smudges of grease on his face and hands.

As for the other man, he was dressed in clean, neat
clothing, his curly black hair close-cropped, his fingernails
free of any dirt and he carried himself with an attitude of quiet
pride.

"Evenin' there, Dan...Jack," Ned called out. "Looks
like you fellas survived another day."

Further conversation came to a halt as all eyes turned
hungrily to watch Bess and Matty bringing heaping platters of
food to the table.

"Oh, Mama, it all smells so goo..ood," Peter said. "You
do keep us going." He straightened up his long, skinny frame,
before his mother could remind him not to slouch.

Bess sat down beside her son and fondly nudged his
shoulder. Meanwhile, Matty hefted an oversize pitcher and
walked around the table filling mugs with lemon water.

"Ain't ya got no other thing for our kids?" asked Sam.
"They won't eat fish."

"No," replied Bess in annoyance, "I don't. And Sam,"
she added, "the right words are 'haven't.' and 'any'. If you're
going to better yourself, you need to learn to speak properly."

Matty grinned. Gramma just doesn't give up, she thought. If she had her way, we'd all be speaking like His Excellency the Governor. Placing the pitcher in the middle of the table, she settled down on the bench next to Bess. While she ate, Matty glanced now and then at the people around her. She knew it was wrong, but she couldn't help feeling resentment at the presence of so many boarders. We shouldn't have to live this way, she thought, having strangers crowding into our house, causing extra work for Gramma Bess and me. Wish Papa hadn't moved us here last year. I miss our cozy rooms in that tenement in northwest Boston — and, having just our family in it.

"Well, Jack, what's the news?" Peter asked. "Did you get the job?"

Jack was slow in responding. "No. I didn't get it. The post office wouldn't give it to me."

"Why not, you're certainly qualified," said Peter. "That notice in the newspaper said they wanted a man who's well-spoken, a good reader, neat in appearance. That's certainly you."

"They said they couldn't hire me because the law won't let them."

"I don't understand."

"It's the government in Washington," Jack replied. "They made a law against black people having anything to do with mail delivery.

"Oh my goodness," Matty piped up, "that's the second one today! Another crazy law against black people."

Peter stared at her. "The second one? What are you talking about?"

Too late, Matty realized she'd put her foot in it. But before she was forced to reply, Fate stepped in to save her.

An elderly black man in shabby, oversized clothing came shuffling into the room. "Bless ya. Bless ya," he called out. With a broad and nearly toothless smile lighting his face, he went around the table, hugging each person and repeating the same 'Bless ya. Bless ya'. Adults across the table from Matty either shrugged in annoyance or gave no response. The children giggled and squirmed. Matty and her family, however, responded warmly, just they as always did.

"Well, Hugger, you're late as usual," said Bess. "Mind you, one of these days you'll arrive to empty platters and have to go to bed hungry."

Hugger kept right on smiling. He drew up a rickety wooden stool and seated himself at the fireplace end of the table. Pointing, he indicated that someone should send the nearly empty platters his way.

Sam leaned forward to talk to Jack. "Whatcha gonna to do fer a job? We all gots to pay our room and board 'round here."

"I don't know, Sam," Jack replied. "I'll find something soon. Maybe now with a war coming, I'll join the Navy and fight the British. I hear the pay's not too bad."

"That's sure gotta be better'n what I get muckin' out stables," Sam said. Rapidly downing the last bite of food, he pushed up from the bench. "Come on, Annie, we'll take the kids out on the bridge, see the sun set."

Poor Annie, Matty thought as she watched them leave. She still acts so fearful, hiding upstairs with those kids whenever Sam is away. It's been almost six months since they came north. Surely, the slave catchers can't still be looking for them.

"Thanks for supper, Bess," said Jack, as he stepped away from the bench and headed for the door. "Please don't worry, folks, I'll find some way to catch up with my rent."

Dan hurriedly finished eating and silently followed Jack out.

When they were gone, Bess turned to Peter. "We can't let Jack's rent slide much longer. He's almost four months behind."

"Ah, don't worry so much, Mama. We'll be alright. I've got a lot of steady customers for my blacksmith work and plenty of horses needing new shoes. And, if war does come, there'll be lots of iron work for the ships."

Bess nudged Matty's shoulder. "You hurry and finish," she said, "so you can start cleaning up here. I've got to put on a fresh apron before I go to my charity meeting. Peter, you ought to shave before you go to your lodge meeting."

"The Masonic Lodge meets tomorrow night, Mama. And, I'm old enough to know when I need a shave, thank you." Peter smiled and kissed his mother's cheek. Then he asked, "How come the African Ladies Charity has another meeting? They had their weekly one two days ago."

"We've got some new problems since then," replied Bess. "Mrs. Jackson died yesterday, leaving her little ones orphaned. We've got to find someone in the neighborhood to take them in."

"Yes," Ned spoke up, "otherwise they might end up in that dreadful almshouse. Just wish this town had an orphanage that welcomed black children."

"On top of that problem," Bess said, continuing as if

she hadn't heard Ned, "several more black folks have come into town and they're in need of a room somewhere. And, they've got to find work as soon as possible. If they don't, you know what might happen to them."

"Yes, I know," said Peter. "The police still keep a close watch on newcomers, especially blacks, it seems. We don't want our people being forced out of town because they don't have work. I'll see if some of my Lodge members can help them."

He and Ned got up from the table and headed outside. Like other men in the neighborhood, they would likely settle on the front steps to enjoy the last of the daylight.

Seeing them leave, Hugger hurriedly swiped his plate clean with a hunk of bread and stood up. He leaned across the table, patted Bess and Mattie's hands while uttering his usual "Bless ya. Bless ya," before heading out the front door. Matty stayed in place on the long wooden bench so that Bess could slide to the far end before getting up.

"That poor old soul," said Bess. "I don't know how Hugger can be so loving after all he's been through. Now Matty," she continued, "when you finish washing the dishes you make sure to dump the water properly. Ned tells me you've been tossing it out the front window and I won't have that."

"But, Gramma, I always look first to make sure nobody's passing by."

"Doesn't matter," Bess responded. "I don't want that muddy mess in front of the house. And besides, it's not respectable. You carry the dishpans out to the middle of the street and then dump the water on the drain."

She started to leave the room and then changed her mind. "Matty, you make sure to stay close to home. When I get back from my meeting we're going to sit down and talk with your papa. He needs to know about your adventuring up the hill today."

Chapter Three

*M*uch later that night, Matty lay in her narrow cot by the open window staring at a clear, star-filled sky and its sliver of a waning moon. Usually such a sight brought sleepy comfort – but not tonight. Turmoil and Despair danced on her pillow.

Ever so slowly, she turned on her side to face the wall. She hoped the new ropes supporting her straw-filled mattress would stay silent. But they groaned anyway. And, would do so until they loosened up a bit. Annoyed, she held her breath and listened. She certainly didn't want to disturb her grandmother's sleep, especially not after that talking-to she'd gotten a few hours ago.

But, across the room in her larger bed, Bess merely continued her soft, wheezy snoring. It's odd, Matty thought, how my small sounds can sometimes wake her, but she'll sleep right through louder noises from outside.

At well past midnight, however, the pitch-dark surrounding neighborhood was mostly quiet. Only now and then was the stillness broken by a yowl and fuss among stray cats or the distant rumble of a late-night carriage down on Cambridge Street.

Matty listened for noises from within the house as she let her mind journey from their first floor bedroom, down the dark hallway and then past the closed kitchen door. Behind that door, she knew the room would have taken on its nighttime appearance. The supper table and other furniture would have been shoved aside to make room for a fold-down bed, one shared by her father and great uncle Ned. Their usual snoring would be muffled by the door and by the thick fireplace wall which separated that room from the back one where Matty now lay.

Continuing on her imaginary journey, Matty climbed steep, ladder-like stairs to the second floor loft to envision the crowd of people sleeping in that low-ceilinged space. Only a tiny window at each end provided light and ventilation. In the back section, Jack, Dan and Hugger would be sprawled on straw-filled mats on the floor. A piece of canvas, hung from the slanted ceiling, separated them from the front area where Sam, Annie and their children lay on their mats. Matty felt badly to realize how dreadfully hot that loft must be now that summer was here.

A sound of Bess shifting on her bed brought Matty's thoughts back to their room and, inevitably, to that unpleasant discussion after supper. *I don't see why Gramma had to tell Papa on me,* she thought with disgust. *Why didn't she just tell me that going up Beacon Hill was wrong and let it go at that?* Closing her eyes, Matty recalled that scene earlier in their kitchen.

+⟩━⟩━⟨+ ● +⟩━⟩━⟨+

"I'm really disappointed in you," Peter said quietly. He and Bess were seated across the table from her. "I just hope you realize now what a foolhardy chance you took," he said.

Matty felt tears coming and looked away. *Why doesn't he holler at me like Gramma does,* she thought, *then I could get mad instead of feeling so awful.*

But she couldn't get angry at her father. She adored him. He was her hero. She knew he never raised his voice, at least not in anger. Whatever blustery winds came his way, he always seemed to meet them head-on with those thoughtful, steady, dark brown eyes and his rich deep voice.

"From now on, Matty," Peter continued, "you are not to leave this house unless you have permission from your grandma or Ned or me. And, you are not to go more than a block away unless one of us is with you."

"Oh, Papa, I won't go up the hill anymore, I promise. And I'll just stay in our neighborhood where it's safe."

Peter leaned forward and looked past a glowing candle to study Matty's face. "You're not a child anymore," he said. "A young girl like you needs to be careful. And, it is not entirely safe for us — here or beyond this neighborhood."

"That's sure the truth," Ned spoke up. He was seated in his usual spot at the window end of the table, smoking his pipe while leafing through an old, tattered copy of Mr. Johnson's *DICTIONARY*. That quirky dictionary was often a source of family fun during after-supper gatherings. Not tonight, however.

"But Papa, you told me we'd be safe when we came to Boston."

"Stop your backtalk, Matty," said Bess. "Listen to what your papa's trying to tell you."

"It's all right, Mama," said Peter. "I don't mind her getting into the discussion." He pushed aside several books and some business papers he had been working on. "We are safer here, Matty, compared to some other places. There's certainly less chance of our being kidnapped and sold back into slavery down South. And, with so many black people in this neighborhood, we can look out for one another.

"But even so," he continued, "there are still dangers.

You discovered one today. Some terrible things have happened to black women alone on the streets, being attacked by white men or gangs of white boys — not so much here as elsewhere ·in town."

"What things, Papa?" Matty's eyes were wide with curiosity.

"Well, I'm not going to go into a lot of detail right now," said Peter, "but you need to be cautious. And anyway, a young girl like you shouldn't be wandering off by herself. You could get a bad reputation."

"Explain to her about the law, Peter," said Bess.

"Which law, Mama?"

Matty spoke up. "Gramma says there's a law against us being on Boston Common."

"Oh, that law," said Peter. "Your gramma's got it a bit wrong. It wouldn't have applied in your case. It only has to do with keeping black people away from the Common at night or during the Sabbath. I'm not sure it's even in effect anymore."

"But why, Papa? Why would they make such a law? And, that law keeping Jack from being a postman, just because of his skin color! That's nonsense!" Matty scowled and folded her arms. "I know white people dislike us, but they shouldn't be able to make laws against us. We're free citizens like them. We're not their slaves anymore!"

"You might think we were," Ned growled, "the way they treat us, trying to prevent us from getting ahead in the world."

"Are there other laws against us?" Matty asked.

"Well, around here, the only official ones I know of," said her father, "are laws preventing us from serving in the militia and from marrying a white person. "But," he added, "when it comes to the government in Washington, that's a different matter."

"Sure is," Ned said in disgust. "With the way things are down there, I guess they could make any law against black folks they want to."

"But not us in Massachusetts," Matty argued. "We're free."

"But more than a million of our people down South are not," said her father. "And think about all our people in other northern states, hundreds and hundreds of them, still in slavery, waiting to be the right age so they can be freed. As far as the Federal Government is concerned, slavery can exist in any state that wants it. And, I don't think free black people are considered rightful citizens. It's true we've managed to get our freedom in this state, but we're a long way from being protected against unjust laws, here or in Washington."

Peter's words seemed to hang in the air. For a moment or so, conversation stopped. The only sounds were the quiet tick-tock of a small clock on the wall and the steady click of Bess's wooden knitting needles. As usual, she had already begun work on woolen socks for next winter.

"So, it's hopeless for us," Matty said. "All that talk about our getting educated, learning to speak properly and seeking respectability, that isn't going to do us any good."

"Of course it's not hopeless!" said Bess firmly. "We're improving our lives every day. Your Papa's got a good job and now that we're taking in boarders we're able to put by a bit of savings. And, look at all the good work that we're accomplishing in our community through the African Society, the

Masons and our church. It's just going to take time to prove ourselves. Once we get white people's respect they'll change their attitude, see that we deserve the same rights they have." Bess took a moment to catch her breath before continuing.

"Mind you, girl, not all white people are unfriendly to us. We've got some kind white neighbors around here. And, don't forget, there were some white folks who helped raise money to build our meeting house."

Looking pleased with herself at setting Matty straight, Bess resumed her knitting. Ned stood up and walked over to the woodpile beside the fireplace. He snapped off a small twig, and began cleaning his clay pipe. He looked thoughtfully over at Bess.

"Seems to me, Sister mine," he said, "we're just spittin' in the wind, trying to change white folks' attitude. Unless they all go blind, our getting respectable isn't gonna change things. I think all of us free black folks would be far better off if we left this country — if we took advantage of Captain Paul Cuffee's offer and went to Africa on his ship."

+>—<+ ● +>—<+

Now, with sleep tugging at Matty's eyelids, she tried to still her thoughts, stop going over and over this upsetting day. But some of her grandmother's comments earlier came to mind. Oh, I don't care what she says, Matty thought. It is hopeless for us. And, all my wishing and dreaming is foolishness. There'll never be a better life for us, no fine, big house in a nicer part of town. No room of my own and lots of pretty clothes. We'll always be stuck in places like this and living with white people's hostility. They'll never let us really belong anywhere!

Before she could stop it, that word, *belong*, took hold, sending her thoughts down a troubling, well-worn path. Never would she forget the day when she discovered she didn't belong anywhere. She had been only five years old.

That afternoon in Portsmouth began so happily, she thought. And, I was so looking forward to our freedom celebration – until Papa spoiled it.

Once again, she saw her small self with her relatives standing in the town clerk's office, watching as they and that slave master, Joshua Warren, signed their freedom documents. Then, later on, in their quarters back of the Warren mansion, sitting contentedly on her father's lap while he explained about those documents.

Vividly, she recalled that scene and her sudden fear at certain of his words.

⊹⊱⋖⊰ ● ⊹⊱⋖⊰

"Matty child, these papers mean that we are now free to leave Portsmouth."

"But Papa, this is our home. Why would we leave it?"

"This isn't our home," he replied angrily. "We don't belong here! We never did. We're only here because some slave trader forced your great grandparents to come here!"

"But…where do we belong, Papa?"

"I don't know yet," he replied.

⊹⊱⋖⊰ ● ⊹⊱⋖⊰

Gosh, Matty now thought, I wonder if Papa really knew how much that scared me, that sudden terrible lost feeling. Then he made things worse, telling me he was going away, leaving me with Gramma and Uncle Ned. Guess I might have made a big fuss if he hadn't so quickly promised to come back for me as soon as possible.

Of course, what really made me feel better was his other promise, that promise he would find a special place for us to live, a place where we could truly belong. And, oh, how I hung onto those promises. Just wish it hadn't taken him nearly four years to keep them — at least the first one. I suppose if I'd been older, I'd have lost hope of ever seeing him again the way Gramma and Uncle Ned did.

Restlessly, Matty shifted her perspiring head on the pillow, trying to find a cooler spot while memories kept flashing by.

There she was with her relatives during those waiting years, continuing to serve in the Warren household, though as *paid* servants. Day after day, with dust cloth in hand, she wandered through elegant rooms of that great mansion, wistfully daydreaming of the future. Never was there any doubt in her mind that one day, when Papa returned, he would take them to a wondrous belonging place — and buy them a house just like the Warren mansion.

Her memories skipped onward to that joyful Christmas Eve nearly four years later when her father finally returned. Not only was he safe and well, he brought happy news that they were moving to Boston where he had found work in a blacksmith's shop. And, if all went well, he hoped to buy that shop when the elderly owner retired.

For a moment or so, Matty thought about their arrival in Boston when she was almost ten years old. When we moved into a tenement near the waterfront in northwest

Boston, I didn't really pay attention to how crowded and run-down it was. I just thought that was only temporary, that Papa would soon buy us a fine new house.

No, all my attention was on having lots of new play-mates and going to that little school for black children in a house nearby. And, oh, the happiness I felt when we began attending church in the new African Meeting House a few blocks away. For the first time in my life, I walked into a public place where no one cast disdainful looks on us. And, wonder of wonders, we were allowed to sit wherever we wished — even in first floor pews.

Echoing in her mind, Matty again heard her delighted words as the family left the Meeting House on that first Sunday morning. "Oh, Papa, I'm so happy you brought us to Boston...this is surely our true, belonging place."

Sudden sounds from Bess now jolted Matty's mind back to the present. Across the room, the woman groaned and rolled on her back, then began snoring loudly. Annoyed, Matty pulled the pillow over her head. Go away memories, she thought. It's silly to keep going back, trying to hold onto that childish belief. And, yet ….

Before sleep finally won out, Matty's last thought came as a prayer. Dear God, I know it's wrong to be so discontent-ed. But I can't help wishing we really belonged *somewhere*. I just hope You don't send us across a scary ocean to find it.

Chapter Four
Thursday, 25 June

*N*o! Absolutely not! I will not have one of those people in my house." Angrily, Mrs. Bainbridge threw down her napkin and stood up from the breakfast table. George, the butler, hastened forth to ease back her chair.

"Now, my dear Amelia," said her husband seated at the other end of the table, "you mustn't upset yourself. We do need an extra servant, just temporarily until the maid is back on her feet. I think Lydia may have a good idea."

"Well, I don't!" replied Mrs. Bainbridge in her soft southern accent. She gathered a filmy white scarf over her plump bosom and set her small mouth in a firm line. "I told you long ago that I would never have anything to do with Negras ever again. And," she added, "it is most improper for you to allow young Lydia a say in such matters."

Reaching into a child's high chair beside her, she lifted out a large, fluffy white cat and cradled it in her arms. "Come along, dear Winston," she cooed, "it's time for our morning walk." With head held high, Amelia Tillford Bainbridge turned and swept from the room.

In the stillness that followed, Mr. Bainbridge resumed reading his newspaper while Lydia fretfully pushed a bit of fried egg around on her plate. Then she reached out and gently lifted a bottom corner of her father's paper. "Papa, dearest," she said, looking up at him with a beguiling smile, "can't you do something? Matty really is such a nice girl and I'm sure she'd be a great help until Tilly's leg gets better. Matty could just do kitchen and back-stairs work. Then she wouldn't be in

Mama's sight at all."

Lionel Bainbridge put down his paper and studied his daughter's face. He always found it hard to deny her anything. Finally, in his crisp Boston accent he said, "I think we need to be mindful of your Mama's feelings on this. Now, it isn't because I share her attitude toward black people. It's just that we don't know anything about that girl."

"But you could find out, couldn't you? Couldn't George go down the hill and talk to people?"

"Sir," George spoke up quietly, catching Mr. Bainbridge's eye for permission to speak. "If you'll excuse my saying, that young girl did behave quite properly yesterday — and she was neat and well spoken. It's possible she is Peter Smith's daughter. He's the blacksmith who shoes our horses and those of other residents along Beacon Hill."

"Yes," said Mr. Bainbridge. "I know of him. He's certainly a respectable, intelligent fellow."

"Oh, please, Papa," Lydia begged, "I just know Matty would do a good job here."

"I don't understand why you're so concerned about her," he responded. "If I put a notice in the newspaper, a suitable person would likely apply in a day or two."

"But Papa, my birthday's coming up and we need help now. Cook is all crabby 'cause she's got so much extra work. And poor George, he can't do everything."

Feeling frustrated, Lydia wondered what else she could say to convince her father to hire Matty. I've got a perfectly good plan in mind, she thought, if only I can make it happen.

"I suppose it wouldn't hurt to make inquiries," Mr.

Bainbridge finally said as he stood up from the table. Adjusting his grey coat over his narrow shoulders, he smiled at his daughter. "It may be a fool's errand, but I'll let George go find out what he can. But mind, Lydia, I'm not making any promises."

By mid afternoon, Lydia was growing impatient waiting for George's return. Alone in her bedroom, she rested her elbows on the dusty sill of an open window while searching the back alleyway. Seeing no sign of George, she idly inspected neighboring backyards.

Her family's house, the last one on the right at the upper extension of Walnut Street, was separated from its neighbor by a narrow strip of land. Then around the corner to the eastward on Olive Street, ran a block of eight tall newly-built brick houses. It was their backyards which now held her attention.

Guess no one wants to brave this awful heat, she thought, as she glanced over deserted yards with their small vegetable gardens, a scattering of linens on clotheslines, neatly stacked piles of fire wood and freshly whitewashed outhouses. Bordering the yards and separating them from the next street north – Pinckney Street – was an open meadow with a stable at each end. Several cows and two fine looking horses were quietly grazing on a thick patch of clover. Now and then, the wind carried small swirls of reddish dust over the area – a continual reminder that, just a block away, the excavation of Monument Hill was still going on. For nearly a year, hundreds of men had been digging away at the huge mound behind the State House, reducing it to make way for new houses. A steady stream of horse-drawn carts carried the dirt down hill to the old mill pond.

"I'll be so glad when they finish that mess," Lydia murmured as she turned away from the window and brushed gritty dust from her elbows. Heaving a deep sigh, she settled down on a large floor cushion and reluctantly picked up her embroidery.

I hate doing this, she thought as she began stitching another tail feather of a colorful peacock. Just because Momma is always embroidering, doesn't mean I should be forced to. Besides, I have better things to do. Longingly, she looked over at her little writing desk and the newly arrived novel, The Vicar of Wakefield, waiting there.

Maybe if I talk to Papa, she mused, I might convince him to tell Mama that reading is much more important for me than sewing. Dear, dear Papa, what would I do without him.

'Little Miss Pink Toes on her little pink pillow'. Suddenly, those words popped into her head and she grinned. He hasn't called me that in a long time, she thought. As usual, the story behind that endearment came readily to mind.

She had arrived in the world as a tiny, sickly infant. Neither her parents nor anyone else in their household believed she would survive. Weighing less than five pounds, she was often carried about on a soft pink pillow. Her mother, too frightened by the child's condition, eagerly turned her care over to a nursemaid. But sometimes it was her father who would take on the nighttime duty of carrying his fretful, crying baby about, gently soothing her with his deep voice. Over and over in singsong fashion he'd whisper, "Little Miss Pink Toes on her little pink cushion." In the morning the servants would find him at his desk in the library with a sleeping Lydia propped before him among piles of papers and books.

Despite the grownups' fears, baby Lydia did thrive. In fact, she eventually grew into a chubby toddler full of mischief and thoroughly spoiled by her papa and the servants. Her mother, however, remained disinterested in the child's care. Though never unkind, Mrs. Bainbridge expressed little concern about her until Lydia came of age for proper schooling. From then on, the girl endured a series of strict tutors and her mother's continual criticism. Lydia's only source of comfort came from her father and from his library with its great store of books and a collection of curiosity items from around the world.

As a professor of natural history at Harvard College, Lionel Bainbridge loved to tell his daughter stories of ancient man and of strange plants and animals. When he could spare time from his work, he and Lydia would sit side-by-side amidst the library clutter, happily escaping everyday cares.

Now, the striking of the tall clock in the downstairs hallway banished her daydreaming. Four o'clock, she thought. Oh surely, George must be back by now. I hope he's brought the news I want. If that girl comes here, I'll have a chance to find out for myself what's really happening on the other side of Beacon Hill. I'm tired of overhearing servants' gossip about Negro people and then having Papa refuse to answer my questions about all that.

Putting aside the embroidery, she opened her door and quietly stepped out into the hallway. She glanced toward her mother's bedroom door to make certain it was closed. Then tiptoeing to the curved stairwell, she peered down and listened. Satisfied that no one was around, she tucked her skirts between her legs, mounted the polished banister and rode swiftly to the first floor.

"My gracious," she whispered with a grin as she smoothed down her dress, "such unladylike behavior!"

Becoming aware of her father's and George's voice beyond the closed library door, she moved closer to listen.

"I went directly to Peter Smith's blacksmith shop," said George, "and it turns out the girl is his daughter. He expressed his thanks for our helping her, but he hastened to say that she would never bother us again.

"And as you instructed, sir, I then told him about your need of a temporary servant and wanting to speak with the girl to see if she would be suitable. He replied that he was uncertain about allowing her to work away from home."

"Did he give a reason," asked Mr. Bainbridge.

"No sir. I told him you would expect a reply by Saturday, that if the girl did not arrive at our kitchen door by ten in the morning, you would look elsewhere."

"Oh, Papa, I dearly hope Matty will come," said Lydia, bursting into the room.

Her father looked up in annoyance. "How often have I told you it's rude to eavesdrop on peoples' conversation !"

"I'm sorry, Papa." Though she said those words, Lydia didn't look particularly sorry as she seated herself in a large wing chair.

"Thank you, George," said Mr. Bainbridge. "You may go now."

"Very good, sir."

For a while all was silent as Lydia worried a loose

thread on the chair's green upholstery and watched her father at his work. He never minded her company as long as she kept silent or found a book to read. But Lydia now broke that rule.

"Papa, when Matty comes, may I be here as you speak with her?"

"No. If the girl does come, I'll talk with her by myself."

"But, what about Mama? Won't she...."

"Now Lydia, you know she's not well. There's no need to bother her with this. Besides," he added, "if I do hire that girl, she'll only be here for a week or so."

Chapter Five
Saturday, 27 June

$\mathcal{T}$raffic on Cambridge Street was settling down to its mid-morning pace as Matty and Ned walked eastward. Gone, or mostly so, was the great rumbling of early morning wagons and carts, the shouting and whistling of farmers and tradesmen urging their horses onward to town markets.

Now, with the change, came well-dressed gentlemen on horseback and a variety of carriages for travelers and Boston's privileged folk. No doubt they were grateful at not having to set foot on the town's manure-strewn streets. But no one, rider or walker could escape the foul odor.

Matty held the tip of her neckerchief to her nose and kept her eyes on where she was stepping. On this day it was most important that her shoes stay clean, her dress un-spattered.

"Guess we're in for a stinking summer, same as usual," muttered Ned. "This town is downright foolish, relying on farmers to come and take that manure away. What with haying season and all, they probably won't come get it before fall."

Arriving at the corner of Belknap Street, Matty stopped and gave Ned a hug. "Uncle, there's no need for you to climb this hill," she said, "I can go on alone."

"All right," he replied, "I'll keep watch from here until you reached the top." He smiled and patted her cheek. "I hope this day goes well for you, child."

Excited, Matty wanted to gather her skirts and run, despite the hot sun and the steep slope ahead. But she restrained herself, knowing that Gramma Bess would question

Ned about her behavior. So, finding a comfortable pace for the long climb, she let her thoughts drift over the amazing turn of events which had set her on this new path.

How can this possibly be? Just three days ago, I was in disgrace. Now here I am heading out on my own, to my first job. And, money of my own – well, the part of the wages I don't have to give to Gramma for savings.

Recalling events of last evening, Matty was still surprised that her father had changed his mind despite her grandmother's strong objections.

+⪢⪤• +⪢⪤+

After supper, the family had settled in the shade of the back porch. Matty sat beside Ned on the edge of it while back of them, her father shared the wash bench with Bess.

For a while, no one said anything. Though they were quiet, the crowded neighborhood certainly was not. The warm evening air was filled with sounds of boisterous children, neighbors' gossiping and laughing.

"Matty," her father finally spoke up, "I had a visitor at the shop yesterday."

Turning around to face him, Matty caught an exchange of glances between him and his mother. Clearly, something was wrong. Bess was in her angry pose with arms folded and a deep frown on her face.

"The butler, George, from the Bainbridges," Peter continued, "he came and talked to me about you. It seems, despite the unfortunate incident that took you there, you made a good impression. So good in fact, that the butler said Mr. Bainbridge wants to speak with you about possible temporary employment – tomorrow morning. It seems their maid has a hurt leg."

"Well, I don't care what that man wants," said Bess. "Matty isn't ready for such a thing. She's getting irresponsible. Just look at what happened on Wednesday!"

"Mama, you and I have already discussed this and I don't agree," said Peter. "I know I was annoyed at what she did. But the more I've thought about it, I don't think punishing her by keeping her so close to home is best for her. This could be a good opportunity to teach her responsibility. After all, she'll be under proper supervision and she'll get good training for future work."

"She can get all the training she needs right here,' said Bess, "where we can keep an eye on her."

Too astonished to speak, Matty simply stared wide-eyed as the argument continued.

"Mama," said Peter, "I'm grateful for what you've done for Matty, raising her and keeping her safe – especially those years when I was away. But she's been so sheltered from the real world, a lot more than other children in our situation."

"I won't have her coming and going up there alone," Bess argued.

"She wouldn't be goin' alone," said Ned, "except for her goin' tomorrow morning. Half the neighborhood goes up there to work in the early hours and most come down together at the end of the day."

"It's a foolish idea," Bess insisted. "She's not ready. There'll be trouble. I feel it in my bones."

"Now, Mama, don't fret your self." Peter reached out and patted her hand. "We don't even know if they'll give her the job."

"I could walk with her part way, tomorrow," offered Ned. "See that she gets safely up to the alleyway back of Olive Street."

"Oh, Gramma, please let me go," Matty pleaded. "I'll be on my best behavior and I'll do just what I'm told. I won't get into any trouble, I promise. And I can give you all my wages."

Ignoring Matt, Bess asked, "What about the work around here, Peter? I can't do it alone."

"I'll get Annie to help you," he said. "It's time she came out of hiding upstairs all day with those kids. The work will do her good."

Bess made no reply. Expressions of doubt and worry played across her wrinkled face. Finally, giving a loud sigh, she heaved herself up from the wash bench.

"Well, I'm not happy about this, not any of it. But if you're going, Matty, there's a lot of things you need to know about before you do." Bess motioned for Matty to follow her back into the kitchen.

+═══+ ● +═══+

Now, as Matty reached the top of Beacon Hill and the alleyway gate, she was sweating and breathing hard. But there was no time for a rest. Boston's meeting house clocks were beginning to strike the hour of ten. Quickly, she straightened her mob cap, smoothed down her skirts and hurried into the alley.

At the Bainbridges' the fence gate stood open, revealing an unusual scene for a Saturday morning. A large featherbed was draped over a clothesline with its drippy wet contents sagging toward the bottom. Nearby, a tall white woman was struggling to launder another such bed. It kept billowing out of the large tub.

Glad I don't have that job, thought Matty. Washing a featherbed is no fun.

"I'm pleased to see you're on time," George called out as he held the back door open for her. Stopping to drawing each of her shoes across an iron boot scraper, Matty entered a well-stocked pantry and then followed George into a large kitchen. There, she was confronted by a scowling white woman who stood by the fireplace.

"What's *she* doin' here?" the woman muttered, glancing over her spectacles at Matty.

"That's Mrs. Dugan, the cook," George said over his shoulder as he continued leading Matty out of the kitchen and into a broad, sun-filled hallway.

"The Missus ain't gonna like one of her kind in this house," the cook called out as George closed the door.

Matty steeled herself against reacting, recalling her grandmother's instructions of last evening. *Now mind, child, you've got to learn to hold your tongue. Don't talk back. You only speak when you're spoken to.*

Reaching the front of the hall, George knocked on the door to the right and then entered the library. "The girl Matty is here, sir."

"Thank you. Come in girl," said Mr. Bainbridge, not bothering to look up. He continued working at his large cluttered desk. George went over to wait by the door.

Shyly, Matty approached the desk and then reminded

herself to stand up a bit straighter. Again, her grandmother's instructions came to mind. *'You remember to show respect to white folks. But don't you go hanging your head. There'll be no more of that'.* Matty quickly put a finger to her lips. She'd almost said 'yes Gramma' out loud.

While Mr. Bainbridge was occupied, Matty looked around the room. What a heavenly place, she thought. All those shelves of books…and more of them piled by the chairs. Must be a copy of every book in the world here.

In contrast, a picture of her family's meager collection of books flashed through her mind. Most of them, worn and tattered, were jammed on a long kitchen shelf and on a shorter one above her bed. If it weren't for Uncle Ned's scrounging, she thought, we probably wouldn't even have those.

Finally, Mr. Bainbridge looked up at Matty. "Have you been told why you're here," he asked.

"Yes, sir, my father explained about it."

"This would only be temporary work, you understand?"

"Yes, sir," Matty replied.

"Our maid fell and injured her leg," said Mr. Bainbridge, "and the doctor insists she must stay up in her room for a few weeks. But in the meantime, household work needs to continue. And also, there's a great deal of extra work in preparation for my daughter's birthday celebration next week."

"Yes, sir, she told me about that," Matty volunteered. "We are almost the same age and I…." She put a hand to her mouth, worried at being too forward.

Ignoring her comment, Mr. Bainbridge continued on.

"George tells me you have had some experience in house-work."

"I grew up working in a fine, big house like this, sir. It was back in Portsmouth, New Hampshire."

"How old were you when you left there?"

"I was almost ten, sir."

Nodding at that, the man sat back in his chair. "If you are hired, Matty, you must arrive here by half past five in the morning promptly and continue work until after supper. You must work quietly and follow instructions without comment. And, you would need to begin training for work today. Can you do all that?"

"Oh, yes, sir. I know I can."

"Well then, wait out in the hall while I speak with George."

Matty carefully closed the library door, but stood close to it and listened. Some of the conversation was muffled by the door, but she did hear Mr. Bainbridge say, "You make certain she does her work out of Mrs. Bainbridge's sight. I don't want my wife getting upset."

"It's not polite to eavesdrop," whispered a voice from above Matty's head. Quickly she stepped back and looked up. There was Lydia, leaning over the stair railing, giving her a broad smile. "It's all right," the girl continued whispering, "I feel sure Papa will hire you."

Before Matty could reply, George opened the library door and stepped out into the hall.

"Come along with me, girl," he said, heading back to the kitchen. "We must discuss your duties."

I guess that means I've been hired, Matty thought as

she quickly followed behind the tall, straight-backed man.

In the kitchen, George seated himself at a small desk located under a window to the left of the fireplace. He had a reserved, proud way about him, but he smiled kindly as he beckoned Matty to come forward. Across the room, Mrs. Dugan looked up from her work and scowled in Matty's direction.

"Now then," said George, "Mr. Bainbridge has decided that you are suitable, provided you follow all instructions properly."

"Oh, goody!" a voice called out. "I can give her a tour of the house."

Matty turned around. There was Lydia, sitting at the top of a narrow, enclosed back staircase.

"Uh… yes, Miss Lydia," George said with some hesitation. "Of course I will need to accompany you. But first I must explain to the girl about her duties. Do you read, Matty."

"Yes, sir," she replied proudly. "I can read — and write, too."

"Good. That will save us time. And, there's no need to address me as 'sir'. You may call me by my first name.

"When you arrive each morning," he continued, "you must have on a clean apron and head covering. Always use the back door and make certain to scrape your shoes well before entering. And, you will make every effort to do your work out of sight of family members, especially Mrs. Bainbridge."

"What about me?" Lydia called down the stairs.

"Well, that doesn't necessarily apply to you, Miss," he said, "but you understand we must respect your father's wishes in this case." Turning back to Matty, he handed her a sheet of paper. "I prepared this list of your everyday duties. Take it with you so you can study it. In addition to those things, you will do whatever Mrs. Dugan instructs here in the kitchen and you will attend to Tilly's needs upstairs."

He hasn't said anything about my wages, thought Matty. Aren't they going to pay me? "Excuse me, sir...uh, George," she said. "Did Mr. Bainbridge mention my wages?"

"Oh, yes, of course. I should have told you. You will receive seventy-five cents at the end of each week."

Without waiting for any reaction from Matty, he stood up and headed for the hallway. "Come along. I'll show you through the house. We must hurry, though," he said, "it will soon be time for the noon meal."

Lydia scampered down the stairway and followed them.

Indicating a closed door just beyond the kitchen, George said, "That is the back parlor where the family has most of its meals."

Lydia quickly reached to open it, preparing to provide a full view, but George was already beckoning Matty toward the front of the house.

"The library you already know about," he said quietly. He then opened a door across the hall from it. "This is the best parlor and back there, through the archway is the dining room."

Matty was given only a minute or so to gaze in wonder at the room's splendid furniture, large portraits, oval mirrors and carpeting in a brightly colored geometric design before George closed the door again. Then he led the way up the carpeted front staircase. Matty was about to follow him when Lydia stepped in front of her and turned around.

"My birthday party will be in that parlor," she said, watching Matty closely.

Matty gripped the railing and tried to control her expression. Up to that point, she'd been letting her feelings show, her excitement at being here, at being in Lydia's company again. Now, there seemed to be something about the girl's attitude that made her feel uncomfortable, uncertain. Is she trying to make me jealous, she wondered.

"Matty," George quietly called down, "you understand you must not use this staircase, except when you're cleaning it."

"Yes, George," she replied, stepping around Lydia.

In the upstairs hallway, George put a finger to his lips for silence. He opened a door to the left of the stairs and said softly, "this is the spare bedroom and the one beyond, at the front of the hall, that belongs to Mr. Bainbridge. Across from there is Mrs. Bainbridge's room."

"And there is my bedroom," Lydia said out loud, "...the one between the back stairs and those leading to the third floor."

"Is that you, Lydia," called a woman's voice from behind Mrs. Bainbridge's closed door.

"Yes, Mama."

"What are you doing out there? Who are you talking to?"

"Nothing, Mama. I was just speaking with George." Lydia grinned at Matty.

"Well, stop lollygagging and bring me your embroidery," the woman called out. "I want to see what progress you're making."

"Yes, Mama," Lydia said. Then she whispered to Matty, "Oh, drat! I wanted to go through the house with you."

George beckoned Matty over to the back staircase. "We better go down to the kitchen," he whispered.

"When will I see the third floor," Matty quietly asked as she followed him down the steps.

"You'll see that when you take a food tray up to Tilly," he replied.

Matty barely reached the bottom of the steps before Mrs. Dugan's grouchy voice called out, "Well, George, ain't you gonna put that girl to work? Tell her to go wash her hands."

Matty saw George frown as he approached the cook at her work table in the center of the room. "Mrs. Dugan," he said, "this is Matty Smith. If you have instructions, please address her yourself — and," he looked the woman in the eyes, "I'm certain Mr. Bainbridge wants her treated with respect."

Mrs. Dugan snorted, but didn't reply. Looking at Matty she pointed across the room. "The sink's over there. And mind you use the soap. Don't just wipe your dirty black hands on the towel."

Nasty old woman, thought Matty. My hands aren't dirty. She approached a worn table against the back wall where wash basins and a filled water bucket waited. Next to the table, Matty noticed a large stone container on a stout wooden frame. There was a small round hole in the bottom of the container.

"What are you standin' there for," Mrs Dugan called out. "Ain't you never seen a sink before? No," she answered her own question, "I don't guess there are any down where you live. Well, just use a basin, then dump the wash water down the sink hole."

Wonder where it goes, thought Matty as she grabbed a chunk of soap. Guess this fancy house has a pipe out to the yard or maybe clear out to the street drain.

"When you're done," said the cook, "come get Tilly's food tray. And mind, don't you dawdle around upstairs."

On the way to the third floor, Matty hungrily inspected the tray. There were two thick slices of buttered bread, a small hunk of cheese, a bowl of strawberries and a mug of cider. My, she thought, the servants eat well around here.

Just as she reached the top landing, the tinkling of a bell sounded. It came from the first room on the left. But when Matty entered the small bedroom she saw no one.

"Come on through the cook's bedroom. I'm back here," called a shrill voice. "High time somebody thought of my needs."

Matty paused in Tilly's doorway, looking for a place for the tray. The small room was a cluttered mess. Near an open window sat a thin, pale- looking young woman with a bandaged leg propped on a stool. Her long, stringy red hair hung down over her crumpled nightgown. The sight reminded Matty of a seaweed-covered rock at low tide.

"Well, for land's sakes!" said Tilly, giving Matty an unfriendly stare. "They really did hire a Negro to do my job. I can't imagine you could possibly do it right. Well, don't just stand there gaping, girl. Put the tray on the bed. And while you're here, see to my chamber pot."

Clenching her teeth, Matty struggled hard not to show

any reaction as she put down the tray. Then, reaching under the bed, she grasped the handle of a covered china pot and drew it out. The stench assailed her nose.

"Mind you don't spill that on your way down," Tilly said in a taunting voice. "And, then you get right back up here to tidy this room."

All the way down the stairs and out to the backyard privy, Matty silently fought her anger. Such mean, nasty people. *Why do they act that way? I didn't do anything to deserve such hatefulness. It's going to be mighty hard holding my temper around them.*

Once again, as if her grandmother was there beside her, Bess's words came to mind. *You just be prepared, Matty. Most likely you'll hear some rude comments about us if you go to work in that house. But it's best if you don't react or reply. No matter how hurtful their words, don't you give them any satisfaction. You just pretend you didn't hear. But mind, now, don't you let anyone take a hand to you. If they do, you leave immediately.*

When Matty came back into the kitchen, George told her, "Never mind about returning that chamber pot, just set it on the stairs for now. Go fetch water to fill up Mrs. Dugan's water barrel. When you're done, refill the wood box and then start scouring those pots and pans." He turned back to his work at a kitchen dresser, assembling china, silverware and linen.

Dutifully, Matty grabbed the rope handles of two buckets and was just starting for the back door when Lydia walked into the kitchen.

"George," the girl said in a commanding voice, causing him to pause at his task. "After Matty is through washing dishes from our midday meal, I want her to come up to my room and give it a thorough cleaning. Mama and Papa's rooms had their spring cleaning before Tilly's accident but mine is still waiting." Waving to Matty, Lydia turned on her heel and marched out into the hallway.

"As you wish, Miss," George patiently called after her.

Chapter Six

"Do you know the proper way to clean a room?" asked George as he and Matty stood in the doorway of Lydia's bedroom. He held a large pile of folded cloths. Matty carried a bucket of water, a mop, and a broom. Lydia was seated at her desk, watching them.

"Oh yes," Matty replied confidently. "First, I cover all the furniture with those cloths and remove the little rugs — I'll take them to the backyard later for beating. I then dust the ceiling and the woodwork and mop the floor. After that I remove the coverings and dust all the furniture."

"That's fine," said George, putting the pile of cloths on a chair. "But, don't forget to wash off finger marks and fly specks on doors and window sills. There's no need to bother about the windows. I have men coming to clean them next week."

George looked at Lydia and hesitated a moment. "Uh… Miss Lydia, perhaps you'd be more comfortable if you left the room for now."

"Oh, that's all right, George," she said, waving off his suggestion. "I'll stay and keep Matty company."

"As you wish, Miss," he replied.

Matty couldn't help noticing George's frown as he left the room. I guess Lydia gets whatever she wants, she thought. Unfolding a large cloth, she began to cover the bed. Lydia quietly closed the door and then hastened to grab one corner of ·the cloth.

"Here, let me help with that," she offered.

"Oh no, Miss. I can do it myself. You don't want to soil your dress."

"Nonsense," replied, Lydia. "I can help you while we have a nice visit. And, you can tell me all about you, where you live and everything."

Matty wasn't sure how to respond so she kept quiet.

"Where do you live down there?" Lydia persisted. "Is it near where the wicked people live? I often hear Tilly and Mrs. Dugan talking about Negro people and what goes on down there. Of course they don't know I'm listening from the top of the back stairs."

What's she talking about, Matty thought in annoyance. We don't live near any wicked people. Smoothing out the dust cover on the bed, she kept her silence as she proceeded to drape other furniture.

"It's all right," Lydia assured her, following her around the room. "You can talk to me. I won't tell anyone. I'd dearly like to be your friend."

Matty wondered about the 'friend' part. That doesn't seem likely with my being a servant and all, she thought. Still, as she looked over at Lydia's eager, smiling face, doubt began to fade. Guess it wouldn't do any harm to answer her questions, she told herself.

"Well, Miss, we live on Butolph Street just a little way up the hill from Cambridge. It isn't an elegant neighborhood like this is, but I don't know of any wicked people living there."

"What kind of a house do you live in," asked Lydia as she plopped herself in the middle of her bed. "Do you have a big family? What do you do for amusement?"

For goodness sake, Matty thought, how do I begin to answer all that? Pondering what to say, she finished covering Lydia's desk and opened the bottom sash of two windows. Matty then wrapped a cloth over a broom and tied the ends tightly. Holding it above her head, she began marching back and forth across the room, sweeping the ceiling to remove any cobwebs and whitewash dust.

Gaining confidence, she decided to start answering Lydia's questions. In short, breathy phrases as she kept on with her arduous task, she described her house and each of her relatives. Occasionally, she glanced at Lydia for her reaction, but was always reassured by the girl's friendly expression.

"As to amusements," Matty said, "we don't have much time for that. There's just too much work to do, especially since we have so many boarders."

"You have boarders," Lydia asked in surprise. "Oh, do tell me all about them."

"Well, right now there are seven of them," Matty began. "There's Sam and Annie and their two little ones — Sassy is two and Nan is almost three. Sam works at a livery stable and Annie, well I guess she'll be helping around our house now that I have a job.

"And then there's Dan who works at the rope factory and Jack who's looking for work. He's such a nice, kind man and handsome, too. And then there's Hugger, but he's too old and lame to do any work."

"That's a funny name. Why's he called Hugger?"

"I guess it's because he likes to hug people." Matty replied with a grin. "I've never heard him called by any other name. He's a peculiar old man who never says anything but

'Bless ya. Bless ya.' Gramma Bess says he's that way because his brain was damaged. He was terribly beaten for many years by his master until he escaped and came to Boston."

"Oh my, how dreadful," Lydia murmured. She looked down at the embroidered bed coverlet showing through its dust cloth and idly began tracing a trailing green vine with her finger.

"Must be awful being poor," she finally said. "But I guess most everyone is, down where you live."

"We're not poor," Matty quickly replied, letting her annoyance show.

"My father is part owner of a blacksmith shop and he brings home good money. We only took in boarders so we could save extra money to buy a house someday."

"I shouldn't have said that, Matty," Lydia apologized. "I didn't mean to offend you."

Matty continued as if she hadn't heard. "And, there are lots of people in our neighborhood who have even more money than we do. They own shops and other businesses in the community and —"

"Oh, my goodness," Lydia suddenly interrupted, brushing frantically at her hair. "You swept cobwebs and flies down on me."

"I'm so sorry, Miss. I didn't mean to." Matty feared Lydia would think she had done that on purpose, considering what she'd just been saying. But Lydia started laughing.

"It's all right," she said, brushing the small bit of fly-caught web out of her hair. "Serves me right for not wearing a cap like yours. Glad there wasn't a spider in that." She shivered, then settled back down to watch as Matty resumed brushing the ceiling.

"Matty," Lydia spoke into the silence, "please do go on talking. There's so much more I want to know. I noticed when you were telling about your relatives you didn't mention your mother."

"No, I didn't," replied Matty. "She died a few days after I was born."

"That's very sad. I'm sorry to hear that." Lydia sounded sincere, but she barely paused before asking another question.

"Your family name, Smith, — that's the same as Tilly's. I don't imagine you'd be related?"

"No," Matty replied. "Smith isn't our real family name. That's just a name my father chose for us."

"He did? Why?"

"Well, Miss, that's a long story," said Matty, finishing the last of her brushing.

"Oh, goody! I love long stories. Do tell me," Lydia pleaded. "And be sure to start from the very beginning." Rolling over on her stomach, she propped her chin on folded hands and gave Matty a warm smile.

Encouraged by the girl's interest, Matty began assembling her thoughts. *This will be my first experience as a storyteller. I hope I can do it as well as Gramma Bess always does.*

"Our family lost its name," she began, "its connection to our ancestors about the time my great grandparents were born. They were born on one of the sugar plantations on the island of Barbados where thousands of Africans were held in slavery. Sometimes, a plantation owner would sell a few of the Africans to passing trade ships or to other plantation owners.

That happened to the parents of my great grandparents. They were sold and sent away to another island. And, neither couple was allowed to take their young babies with them."

"What a *dreadful* story," Lydia exclaimed.

Matty looked startled. "Uh…I'm sorry, Miss. I didn't mean any harm. I just thought you wanted to —"

"No, no," interrupted Lydia. "It's all right. It is a shocking story, but I do want to hear it. I want to know about all that."

Uncertain if she really ought to continue, Matty kept her head down and began mopping the floor. Hoping to divert Lydia's attention, she said, "there's a lot of gritty dust in here."

"I know it," Lydia agreed. "Isn't it awful? Even when we keep the windows closed it manages to seep in on windy days. It's from all that digging going on back of the State House."

"You have the dust and we have the smell." Matty grinned.

"Smell?"

"Yes, Miss," Matty replied. "They've been dumping that dirt into the mill pond and it's become a really bad smelling swamp."

All was quiet for a few moments. Then Lydia said, "Won't you please go on with your story, Matty? I would really like to hear it."

And so for a while, as Matty continued with her work, she shared some of her grandmother's stories concerning the family and their long enslavement. Beginning with two unfortunate, unrelated babies who were left behind, Matty told of their being taken in by other families. Taba, as the baby girl was named, was given to one family and the baby boy, Jube, was given to another.

"They were never told anything about the parents they had lost," she said, "not their names or anything about where they came from in Africa. Then, when Taba was about sixteen and Jube was nearly a year older, they suffered the same fate as their parents. They and four other boys and girls were sent down to the plantation wharf and sold to a sea captain from New Hampshire."

"What a terrible thing," murmured Lydia.

"It certainly was," Matty replied. "My grandmother said they were terrified and they had to endure a dreadful voyage north. They were locked down in a small, dark, cramped space in the cargo hold and seldom allowed up on deck. What with seasickness and bad food, they were in terrible shape by the time the ship docked in Portsmouth, New Hampshire. That was on a snowy day in February of 1730.

"They didn't have winter clothing so the six young people huddled together on the wharf while, one by one, they were sold at auction. Gramma Bess told me that Taba and Jube had become quite fond of one another on the voyage. Jube even gave her a special name. He called her his 'Pretty Bird'. They wanted to stay together and become husband and wife, but they feared they would be sold to different masters, never see one another again.

"For a change, though, Fortune was kind. Both of them were sold to a Captain McIntire who owned a big mansion house just up the hill from the wharf. My great grandfather got to keep his name which was put on the sale document, but when Taba told the clerk her name was Taba Pretty

Bird, Captain McIntire laughed and told the clerk to write down the name 'Dinah', instead."

"How mean to take away even her name," said Lydia. "Was the Captain cruel to them later on?"

"I don't think so, from what I've been told. But he did keep a whip that hung in the downstairs hallway."

"Were the other young people on the ship sold to plantation owners?

"No, there were no plantations there. They probably were sold to owners of other big mansions in Portsmouth or to farmers.

"Anyway," Matty went on, "Taba and Jube lived in a small wooden building attached to the back of the mansion. They worked very hard and the only rest they got was late at night and a few hours on Sunday when they were forced to go to church with the McIntires. Well, not with them. They had to sit up in the gallery."

"That's where all the Negro people sit in our church," commented Lydia.

Well, they certainly don't in ours, Matty thought in disgust. But she refrained from arguing the point.

"Were there lots of slaves in that town," Lydia asked.

"Not more than about fifty at that time, but they were so scattered around the area they seldom saw one another. I've been told that was one of the most painful things for Africans in New England. They often felt so alone, so cut off from the people they knew, from African ways of doing things and their religion. Their white owners forced them to give up most of that."

Wondering if she'd said too much, Matty stopped talking and began uncovering furniture. She took one of the covers to the open window to give it a good shake. Deciding to join in the effort, Lydia grabbed a cloth and went to the other window to shake it. Giggling, she snapped the cloth at Matty. Surprised, Matty laughed and gave a returning snap with her cloth. Soon, the two girls were traipsing back and forth to the windows, shaking cloths and giggling at one another.

Suddenly, Lydia put a finger to her lips and signaled for them to draw back from the windows. "We better be quiet so we don't wake Mama."

"Is your mama suffering from an illness?

"No, not exactly," replied Lydia. "She just stays in her room a lot of the time." Seeming reluctant to give further explanation, she climbed back up on the bed.

Must be something peculiar about Mrs. Bainbridge, thought Matty, some reason why they don't want me to see her.

Carefully re-folding the dust covers, she piled them on the floor and then began giving each piece of furniture a thorough dusting.

"What happened to your great grandparents later on?" Lydia asked. "Did they have a lot of children?"

"No. Just a set of twins. But they were worried about having them."

"Why?"

"They were always fearful about their future, of their family maybe being separated, especially Taba. She often had nightmares seeing herself down on that wharf again, being taken away from Jube and sold to some other master. Once the twins were born, she and Jube worried that one day when the children were a little older, they might be sold away."

"Oh, Matty, that is so awful," said Lydia, her eyes glistening with tears. "Please tell me those children weren't sold away."

"No. Old Mister Fortune was kind again," smiled Matty. "Captain McIntire and his wife took a great likening to Bess and Ned – that's what they named the twins. They're my grandmother and great uncle, now," she added.

"At first, the McIntires took a special interest in them, maybe because they hadn't any children of their own. They made sure the twins had good care and training. Mrs. McIntire taught them to speak proper English. She was really strict about that. Later on, she and her husband taught them to read and do a bit of arithmetic.

"Of course, that education just made my great grandmother Taba more fearful. She kept telling Jube, the McIntires were only doing it so that later they could sell the children for a better price. But, it turned out she needn't have worried. The children just grew up there, working in that mansion same as their parents.

"There did come a time, though, — much later on — when it looked as if some of the family might be sold away."

Suddenly, a knock came at the door and George put his head in. "Excuse me, Miss Lydia," he said and then spoke to Matty. "I don't know what's taking you so long. By now, you certainly should have finished your work in here." Not waiting for a response, he told her, "Gather up your cleaning things and go down stairs. There's a rain storm coming. You go to the back yard and bring in the featherbeds. Then take them up to the third floor storage room and lay them out to finish drying. After that, get back to the kitchen and help Mrs. Dugan."

Chapter Seven

$\mathcal{B}$y early evening, with the last of the supper dishes dried and put away, Matty headed for home down Belknap Street. And this time she was not alone. Now and then she greeted or waved at people she knew, mostly black women and girls returning home from work in other houses of the well-to-do.

That rain storm, earlier, had been much too brief. It merely dampened the ground, leaving trees, greenery and people begging for a good cooling off. Despite being hot and tired, Matty was feeling elated, looking forward to telling her family all about the new job.

Finally, as she turned the corner onto Butolph Street, she saw her father and Uncle Ned in the distance, sitting on the front steps. Bess was at the open window, comfortably leaning on the sill.

Drawing nearer, she heard her father call out, "It looks like you got the job. How did it go?" He patted the step beside him and Matty gratefully slumped down.

"Oh, Papa, it was wonderful. And…a bit awful, too."

"Whatever do you mean?"

"Well, the wonderful part was seeing Lydia again and seeing her truly beautiful house. It's even more beautiful than where we used to work in Portsmouth. And, the furniture! You should see how lovely it is, so elegant and shiny. The tables and chairs dance on tiptoe, not on those paws and claws like the Warren's furniture did."

"Peter, your daughter's gone daft," said Ned with a laugh. "Imagine, furniture dancing about!"

"I just mean they look that way," Matty explained, "because they have long, thin legs that narrow down at the bottom. And, there are lots of looking glasses and brass candleholders and a pianoforte. And, Uncle Ned, they have a library — a whole room filled with books, magazines and newspapers. Can you imagine that?"

"Oh, my," Ned sighed, "that must truly be heaven."

"That might be for you," muttered Bess, scowling at her brother, "but that's too much of a distraction for Matty. A proper young lady shouldn't be reading just any old book. Young men don't like a girl who's too bookish in her conversation."

Eager to change the subject, Matty said, "Gramma, you should see the kitchen up there! You would love it. It's so big and it's got all sorts of new cookery pans and things. And, beside the fireplace there's something called a stewing stove. It's these three little brick wells with hot coals at the bottom and you put kettles into the wells and while the food is cooking, tin pipes carry all the smoke up through the chimney."

Matty caught her breath before hurrying on. "And, you know what? I didn't have to carry the dirty dishwater out to the street. I put it in a sink and it just drained out of sight. Oh, Papa, I dearly wish we could have a kitchen like that someday."

"You and your wishing," said Bess, shaking her head. "All that does is make you unhappy. You need to accept what is and be grateful for that."

"Mama, don't step on her dreaming," Peter said quietly. "There'd be no making things better if we didn't dream. We'd never have come to Boston if I hadn't been dreaming of a better life for us."

"I know that," Bess agreed. "It's just that I don't like the child being so discontented."

Wish she wouldn't keep calling me 'child', Matty thought with annoyance.

"Tell us about that other part, Matty," Ned asked, "that 'bit awful part' you mentioned."

"Well…you were right, Gramma," said Matty, turning around to look up at Bess, "about having to put up with white people's nasty remarks. The Bainbridges' cook, Mrs. Dugin, and their maid, Tilly — the one with the hurt leg — they never had a kind word for me and they looked at me all the time as though I were some dreadful creature. It's awful working around them. I'm glad I'll only be there for a short time."

Bess shook her head in sympathy. "I know that's disheartening, but if you're going to work in such houses you'll have to learn to deal with that." Seeing Matty's woebegone expression, Bess changed the subject. "Are you hungry, child? Did they feed you?"

"That was another bad part," Matty replied. "I thought I was going to get a nice midday meal, but Mrs. Dugan just gave me slice of bread and told me to take a cup of water with it. I hardly had time to eat it before she made me get back to work. When supper time came she handed me a tin plate with some fatty bits from the ham and half a boiled potato. She wouldn't let me sit at the table, told me to go sit on the back step. Later, when she wasn't looking, I threw away those fatty bits."

"Shameful way to treat you," said Bess, moving back from the window sill. "Well, you come on in. I'll get you a bite to eat before you go to bed.""

Inviting aromas reached out to Matty as she entered the dimly lit kitchen. On the table, in the light of a single candle, she saw several small crocks of baked beans, rounds of ginger bread and a large meat pie. In spite of her mood, she smiled. Gramma never fails to follow the rules, she thought. She's done her usual Saturday task, preparing for the Sabbath. Nice to know tomorrow will be free of unnecessary work.

Sitting down at the table, she gratefully accepted a bowl of milk, some cornbread and a generous hunk of cheese which Bess placed before her.

"Did they work you very hard, child?"

"Not exactly," Matty replied. "It's just that they kept me going all the time. I did have some fun talking with Lydia while I cleaned her room."

"What did you talk about?"

"Oh, just things. She had a lot of questions about us, where we live and all."

For a moment, Bess looked thoughtfully at Matty. "You know, you'd be wise not to be too talkative with that girl, too trusting. It's best to keep family matters at home."

"I know," replied Matty, looking away. Guilt pinched her. Maybe I did talk too much, she thought, but I don't think I did any harm. And surely Lydia would keep her promise, not tell anyone about what I said.

With the next thought, Matty's appetite vanished. What if Lydia told Mrs. Dugan and Tilly. They'll be laughing and making fun of me when I go back on Monday.

"Gramma, do you mind if I don't finish all this? I'm not as hungry as I thought. I'm pretty tired."

"That's all right," said Bess. "You go along, get a good night's sleep.

Quietly, Matty made her way down the narrow hallway to the back bedroom. Over head, she heard the usual sounds of Sam and Annie settling their children for bed. A silence from the area back of there suggested that the other boarders were likely elsewhere, enjoying the leisure of a Saturday night.

Around her, the house felt hot and stuffy despite open windows and doors. And, adding to the discomfort, there was a damp musty odor coming up from the cellar. Must be more puddles on that dirt floor, Matty thought. Stupid rainstorms!

Entering the bedroom, she undressed in the dark. Clothed only in a cotton shift, she lay down on top of the covers. Wish I could light a candle and read a while, she thought, take my mind off things. But that would only bring in the bugs.

Staring into the darkness she silently scolded herself. Why was I so foolish, chattering away to Lydia, answering her prying questions? She's probably told Tilly and the cook everything I said. It's going to be awful going back there.

I suppose I could refuse to go, but how would I explain that to Gramma Bess? And if I do quit, I won't get a reference for another job and then I won't have any money of my own. And, I'll just be stuck here all the time. Oh, I've got to stop thinking about all that or I'll never get to sleep!

Thank goodness, tomorrow is Sunday. She relaxed and smiled at the thought. We'll be going to our African Meeting House. How I dearly love that place.

Chapter Eight

*A*s usual, Sunday arrived in quiet. It came as a blessed relief to town residents, especially those living in busy commercial neighborhoods. By long-standing law, Boston traffic was limited to sedate, church-going carriages. Only a U.S. Mail wagon or some conveyance on an emergency was permitted to disturb the peace.

In her narrow cot, Matty lay listening to what few sounds broke the morning stillness. High above, seagulls were calling to one another and in the back yard a flock of sparrows twittered and fussed over their morning tidbits. Near by, she heard several neighbors quietly talking as they went about their early routine.

I hope Gramma Bess stays asleep a bit longer, Matty thought. I could use a few more winks. But it wasn't her grandmother who spoiled that idea – at least not right away. No, it was her much too busy mind over-ruling her still tired body. Like delighted little demons, last night's worries and imaginings danced once again behind her closed eyelids.

Whatever will I do about Monday? How can I possibly endure Mrs. Dugan and Tilly laughing at me, making fun of what I told Lydia. Oh, why was I so naïve and trusting of that silly girl!

From across the bedroom, came a soft groaning sound as Bess eased herself out of bed and slowly came to a standing position. Not wanting to watch, Matty kept her eyes closed. Must be awful getting old, she thought.

"You can't fool me, child," Bess spoke up. "I know you're awake, so move along. Don't dawdle. There's plenty of chores even if it is the Sabbath."

"Yes, Gramma."

"Did you finish sponging those dirt marks off the back of your best dress?"

"I meant to, but —"

"No 'buts'. You get right to it after breakfast. I won't have you going to church looking a mess."

Except for the boiling up of a pot of coffee, breakfast was a minimum of work, a pick-me-up thing. Everyone helped himself to cold food and any dishes used were neatly stacked for washing until after the supper meal. As for their midday needs (the nooning at church) Bess packed a large basket with a cold meat pie, cheese, ginger cake and a small jug of lemon water.

By half past nine, the Smith family and most of their boarders were ready to head for the meeting house. Bess noticed that Dan was not among the group.

To no one in particular, she commented, "I suppose Dan is still up there sleeping. I just wish he'd start going to church with us...make some effort to be sociable and better himself."

As usual, Bess stood by the front door, inspecting her family's appearance. "Peter, you always do us proud," she said, looking at her son's neat attire.

Despite the warm temperature, he was wearing a black wool jacket over a white shirt with white neck cloth. Gray wool trousers and well polished boots completed his outfit. Bess wore a plain, high necked black dress with a white kerchief around her shoulders. Her curly gray hair was mostly hidden by a tightly wound red and yellow scarf.

Turning her attention to Matty and Ned, Bess looked less pleased. "That dress doesn't fit you anymore," she said, eyeing Matty's green and white checked gingham dress. "It's tight and you're getting too tall for it. And, Ned, you certainly need a new shirt."

"Nothing wrong with this shirt," he responded. "It does have some patches, but it's clean." He picked up their food basket, preparing to lead the family out the doorway. He had chosen to dress casually with just the long sleeve white shirt and well worn black trousers. His shoes, however, were as neatly polished as Peter's boots.

Gramma is such a fusspot, Matty thought. Uncle Ned looks quite respectable. Stepping up beside him, she took hold of his free hand and gave him a big smile. He winked in return as they went out and began walking down street.

Once the group reached Cambridge Street, it was joined by many other people of color walking eastward. Just beyond Russell Street some of them turned into an alleyway leading up hill. Bess, however, always insisted that her family proceed in proper fashion to Belknap Street, then walk up a short distance and turn into May's Court, the first open way on the right.

There, just a few houses away, towering over the narrow dead-end street, stood a large, rectangular brick building — the African Meeting House. Its windows gleamed in the morning sun as if lighting a pathway for church-goers. From the street and several alleyways, people were streaming toward it. Here and there, some paused to greet one another before entering its doorway

Matty felt a surge of pleasure just as she always did

when coming upon this building. More and more, she had come to think of the African Meeting House as her belonging place — an unfailing shelter from the hostile world beyond its doors. It was here she came not only for church, but for community gatherings, celebrations, and also for school during the last four years. She always felt proud knowing that she had been among the first students to attend a new school for black children in the Meeting House basement in 1808.

Now, climbing the circular staircase to the floor above it, she and her family proceeded to their assigned pew in the middle of the spacious, high-ceilinged room. Peter waited while Bess, Matty and Ned filed in. Then he took a seat beside them. Their boarders — Sam's family and the rest — found seats at the back where no one was required to pay a yearly rent for a pew.

Bess immediately bowed her head, but Matty was too busy looking around the room. Nearby pews were filling in and up in the gallery a few people had, by their own choice, taken seats there. Several rows in front of the Smiths, two well-dressed families of color, the Thompsons and the Osborns entered their pews. Among them, two girls, Matty's former school mates, smiled and waved at her.

She returned the greeting, but a small pang of envy dulled her pleasure. We should be sitting up there, if only Papa could afford the higher rental fee. Well, maybe someday he can. And then, I shall have a fine new dress and a new bonnet for every Sunday.

Oh, you silly thing, her conscience scolded, you should be happy with what you have. Think of all the folks in the pews back of you and up in the gallery who can't afford to sit where you do or maybe even have a single coin for the collection plate.

"Matty, stop looking around," whispered Bess. "Quiet your mind and prepare."

Unsure what 'prepare' really meant, Matty tried to keep as still as possible. Her mind, however, was far from quiet. Nor was the room quiet. In contrast to the reserved, New England-taught church behavior practiced by Matty's family and many others in the congregation, there were quite a few people following a different practice. Here and there, folks were joyfully greeting and hugging one another. Matty knew from hearing Bess talk that those folks had come from the West Indies and the South where African culture managed to survive. They had not lost the liveliness and spontaneity of their ancient religious traditions.

Wish I could behave as they do, Matty thought. I think we all should show the happiness we feel about being together in this place.

Gradually, people settled down and then grew silent as the Reverend Tobias Jennings calmly walked down the center aisle. He stepped up onto the platform of the open pulpit and gave everyone a welcoming smile. Smiling back, Matty thought once again how much this pale brown-skinned man resembled her Uncle Ned. Except for small spectacles perched low on his nose, the minister had the same broad features with curly white sideburns below his balding head. And, he had Ned's same penetrating, but kindly way of looking at a person as if he knew exactly what she or he was thinking.

"Before we begin," said the minister, "I have just one announcement. At seven o'clock this evening, the July 14th committee will meet in the school room downstairs. This will be the fifth year our church has celebrated the anniversary of the ending of the slave trade by Britain and our country and Denmark. Anyone wishing to help organize the parade or other festivities, please come to the meeting."

Raising his arms, he then intoned, "My friends, let us give praise unto Almighty God for this new day and for safely gathering us together in this place once more. Brother Smith will now tune the first hymn."

Proudly, Matty watched as her father walked up front and signaled everyone to rise. Accompanied by a violinist, Peter sang alone the first line of Isaac Watts' hymn, 'Love to God and Our Neighbor'. The congregation then joined his rich baritone voice in repeating the line. Following old New England tradition, Peter, as official hymn tuner, led the singing in that way through the next three stanzas. Here and there, a few voices added harmony, some seeming to take a musical journey of their own. But always, those wandering voices came back to blend and mold themselves into a joyous resolution.

Matty happily sang along, feeling the sounds touch her, even to her bones. I wish the whole service were this way, she thought as the hymn ended and they all sat down. I'd like it to be full of music instead of those long prayers and a sermon even longer.

But, wishing was useless. Ahead of the congregation on that increasingly warm, humid morning was the usual service of two hours — perhaps more, if the minister so decided. After a pause for a mid-day meal, there would be another lengthy service. Of course, elsewhere in most Boston meeting houses, things were much the same. Tradition was slow to change. As Reverend Jennings began addressing the congregation, Matty settled back, trying to get comfortable on the hard wooden bench.

"My dear friends," the minister said, "I know your hearts are sorely troubled today, now that President Monroe has declared war on Britain. And, I know that brings fear and uncertainty which only adds to the many burdens we continue to face in our homes and in this community."

As he went on speaking, Matty urgently whispered, "We're at war, Papa? When did that news come?"

"Two days ago," he whispered.

"But, Papa —"

"Shush, not now. We'll talk about it later."

Reverend Jennings continued, "… as we turn our minds to prayer, perhaps some of you may feel the need to speak of a worry or burden you have so we may include that in our prayers. I invite you to do so now."

From here and there, came voices speaking of personal problems and illnesses. Then one voice, a man in the gallery, spoke out much louder than others.

"Preacher, we needs to pray for a quick end to this war. Then Captain Cuffee can bring his ship into port and get us to Africa. I don't want my family stayin' in a country that's hostile to us. There's just no future here for black people."

"Oh no, Reverend," said another man who stood up near the front of the room. "Brother William is wrong in his praying…at least partly so. He's right about the war, but I believe he's wrong about us leaving here. This is our country, same as the white folks. Most of us were born here and some of our men fought and died to free this country from the British King. And, mind you, it's wrong to leave while so many thousands of our brothers and sisters are still suffering in slavery."

"I don't think we'll have any choice," another voice quickly chimed in. "If rumors are true, the government's gonna force all of us free blacks to leave this country."

"Please, please," the minister interrupted, "please remember where we are. Put aside your arguments for another time. All of you have shared important matters with us. Now let us open our hearts to prayer and seek God's guidance."

Though it took a few moments for people to settle down, the rest of the service proceeded without further incident. For her part, Matty struggled hard to pay attention, not let her thoughts pursue those upsetting topics the men had raised.

Throughout the prayers, the hymns, of course, and Bible readings, she was mostly successful. But once the sermon was under way and the minister's explanations of scripture got more complex for her, Matty's concentration failed.

Surely, she thought, the government won't force us to go to Africa. I want to stay here. Well, maybe not here, but some place nice in America. There must be a place for us, one where we'd be safe and away from prejudice, maybe out in the western territory. We could start a whole new town, build fine houses and a school. And, I might even become the teacher.

That fantasy lasted but a moment before another thought intruded. It was a question, one that plagued her often. Why? Why are white people so hostile to us just because of our skin color? How can people like Mrs. Dugan and Tilly be so hateful to me? Surely they're taught the same things we are in church – 'love thy neighbor', 'we're all God's children'. Why don't they see how wrong their attitude is?

Matty shifted a bit on the wooden bench. Its narrow seat was cutting into the back of her thighs. Bess reached over and tapped Matty's hand. "Sit still," she whispered. "Stop twisting your handkerchief and pay attention."

In response, Matty sat up straighter, focusing her eyes on the minister and on an old fashioned hourglass that stood on the pulpit beside an open Bible. Always a source of fascination, Matty watched that glass as the sand from the top globe slowly filled the bottom one. Wish I could hurry that sand along, she thought. I need to stretch my legs and my stomach's begging for food. And, I really need to talk to Papa.

A while later down in the basement school room, Bess began uncovering their nooning basket. "For Heaven's sake, Matty," she said. "Stop your chatter and help me with this food. And, stop pestering your father with questions."

Matty and her grandmother were standing in front of a row of long desks which stretched across the middle of the room. On a bench behind the first desk sat Peter, Ned and several of the boarders. At desks back of them were seated other families and individuals who were also uncovering their food baskets.

Though the Smith family could just as easily have gone home for the nooning, it was Bess who insisted they have it here. For her, these Sunday occasions were not only a time to socialize, they were an opportunity to collect information for her African Ladies' Charity. As head of the group, she would report on anything told to her or overheard regarding needy black people in the community.

Responding to Bess's comment, Matty said, "Well Gramma, I just wanted to know what was going on in church, what those men were talking about…and the war and all."

Peter laughed. "That's my daughter, always so curious. I'll bet your mind was going like a mill wheel in a flood during church."

"Her mind should have been nowhere, but on the service," Bess complained." She handed Matty a thick slice of cold meat pie on a square of cloth, indicating that it be served to Ned.

"Well," said Peter, "we might as well get some of your questions out of the way now. No, I don't know what's going to happen with this war or how bad it'll get."

"Will British soldiers come to Boston like they did before," Matty asked as she passed him the jug of lemon water.

"I don't know, but we certainly hope not." He took a swig from the jug and passed it to Ned.

"Now, let's see," Peter continued. "You were asking me something about the slave trade law as we were coming down the stairs. That law just prohibits British and U.S. ships from transporting enslaved Africans to this country and other places."

"I know that, Papa," Matty said impatiently. "What I want to know is why didn't our government just put an end to slavery at the same time?"

"That's a good question," replied Peter. "It's one I used to wonder about until I did some reading and talking with people. The answer is kind of complicated."

"No it's not," growled Ned. "It all boils down to money. Always does. I think most of this country would have gone broke if they'd suddenly set all of our people free."

"That's the gospel truth," said a very elderly man seated at the desk behind them. He and others had stopped their conversations to listen in.

By now, Matty had finished handing out food and she took a seat at the far end of the bench. Her share of the meat pie looked inviting, but she decided to delay that first bite. There was still one more burning question on her mind. Leaning forward to catch her father's attention, she asked, "Papa, why is the government going to force us to go to Africa?"

But it was Ned who again put forth an answer. "It's because they don't want us stirring up trouble among our brethren down South — or maybe getting organized with other folks to force an end to slavery. Government men likely weren't pleased when our African Society published that pamphlet against slavery a few years ago."

"Now, now," Peter spoke up forcefully. "The government is not going to make free African people leave. That's just a rumor."

"You know," said the same elderly man sitting behind them, "we've been talking for a long time about leaving on our own, trying to find the money, figure some way to get to Africa. Best as I can recall..."

Oh dear, thought Matty, we're in for one of Mr. Brown's long speeches.

"...it was Prince Hall," Mr. Brown continued, "the man

who got our Masonic Lodge going here during the Revolution. He was the one who started the idea. After the war, he and other free Africans got up a petition asking the Massachusetts government for money to help us go to Africa. But the government said no. Since then, there's been various schemes by black folks wanting to leave.

"And," he kept on, "I don't think it's just a rumor about the government. I suspect there are men in Washington right now who're figuring out some way to get us free blacks out of this country. Now mind you, I want to —"

"It's wrong to give up and leave this country," interrupted a man near the back of the room. "I said so before."

His interruption caused other people to speak up, some in agreement and others not. What was normally a pleasant nooning now became a room full of argument. It continued until the ringing of a hand bell summoned everyone to afternoon church service.

As Matty climbed the staircase behind her father, she whispered, "I'm sorry I asked so many questions, Papa. I didn't mean to cause arguments."

"It's not your fault, child. If you hadn't spoken up, somebody else would have. With the war starting, that just makes folks even more upset and fearful about our future."

As they reached the top of stairs, Matty asked, "Are you thinking about taking us to Africa...after the war, I mean?"

"It's a possibility," her father replied. "But I don't really know the answer right now. I need to think a lot more about it. Guess the war will give us plenty of time for that."

Chapter Nine
Monday, 29 June

*W*hatever is the matter, child? Are you ill?" Bess peered closely at Matty's face as they were standing by the open front door a little past five o'clock in the morning.

"No, I'm all right Gramma." Anxious to be off to work, Matty tugged on her mob cap, pulling it further down over straying curls. Wish I didn't have to wear this stupid thing, she thought.

"Well, what is it?" Bess persisted. "You've been walking around here ever since yesterday as if you have the whole world on your shoulders. Frowns spoil your pretty young face."

"It's hard to smile, Gramma, with so much wrong in the world."

"Nonsense! You take everything too seriously. If it's the war you're fretting about, that's the men's concern. We'll be all right." She patted Matty's cheek fondly. "Now you go along to your job. And remember, don't take a shortcut across those fields at the top of the hill. Only use Belknap Street for coming and going. That way you'll be safe."

"Yes, Gramma," Matty mumbled as she went down the steps.

"Head up, child," Bess called softly, "and straighten your shoulders. Take a little pride in yourself."

"Yes, Gramma," Matty mumbled again. It's not just the war I'm worrying about, she thought. It's what might be waiting for me at that house on the hill. And, I dearly wish she'd stop calling me *child!*

Despite the early hour, there were quite a few people on the street. Noticing that, Matty felt her spirits lift a bit. *I'm part of the adult world now. Finally, I have a job — away from home.*

Glancing at black people hurrying by, she was aware that most of them were likely heading for low-paying jobs. Though Fortune had smiled on some, enabling them to create small businesses in the neighborhood — barbers, caterers, dressmakers, shop keepers and craftsmen — most others could only find menial work as house servants, laundresses, dock workers, stable hands and the like.

Now, as Matty trudged up Belknap Street she noticed some of the black women carrying bundles of clean laundry in their arms or atop their heads. Eyeing the bundles perched high, she smiled to herself. *Gramma Bess would certainly approve of those women's straight backs.*

Her smile, however, quickly faded. She knew that such bundles likely represented extra work, a bit of extra income for the women. House cleaners by day, they would return home at night with a load of their employer's soiled laundry. Once washed, those fine clothes and linens would often be safeguarded by hanging them on lines strung across the women's small kitchens and bedrooms.

Oh my, Matty suddenly thought, *I don't want that to be my life. I don't want to follow their same 'housework' path. There's just got to be something better for me, something important!*

Turning into the alleyway leading to the Bainbridges, she lifted her head and firmed her jaw. *I don't know if Lydia has betrayed me but if she has, I'll just have to face it. I am not* going to let Mrs. Dugan's and Tilly's nastiness chase me away.

About an hour later, as Matty was scrubbing the last of the front steps, she began to relax and breathe a bit easier. So far, there'd been no unusual comment from Mrs. Dugan or anyone else. Dropping her brush into the bucket, she took up a cloth and proceeded to dry off the granite surface.

"Don't know why I had to do this," she mumbled. "These steps weren't dirty at all. In fact, I doubt they ever are." She paused to look around at the front sidewalk with its clean, smooth stone slabs glistening in the morning sun. Beyond there, the neatly arranged cobblestones of the little courtyard end of Walnut Street were also free of any dirt. Down at the corner, Olive Street appeared just as clean. Guess the city pays better attention to streets up here, she thought. Or these rich folks pay a cleaner.

"Matty," George quietly called out from the open front door. "What's taking you so long? Finish that up and get on with your other work. I want you away from here before the Bainbridges come down for breakfast."

All of a sudden, Winston the cat appeared and slipped between George's legs. "Murrrow," came his gravelly voice as his fat white body came to a halt in front of Matty.

"Quick! Grab him!" said George. "Mrs. B. will be furious if he gets away."

Matty took hold of the cat and stopped him. With that, he turned and viciously scratched her left arm. Coming to her rescue, George grabbed Winston by the scruff and locked him in his arms.

"Sorry about that," he said, sounding quite concerned. "Gather up your things and go around to the back and I'll attend to your arm."

In the kitchen, Matty sat quietly on the bottom step of the back stairs while George gently tied a strip of cloth around the painful scratches. "Try to keep that arm away from any dirt," he said.

"Well, land sakes," Mrs. Dugan called out as she stood by the worktable, "how's she gonna do her work around here? We don't need another invalid in this house!"

"I can do my work," Matty responded firmly. "My arm won't be a problem." Turning away from Mrs. Dugan's hostile stare, she withdrew a slip of paper from her pocket – the one listing her everyday duties. "I've finished most of the downstairs work on this list," she told George, "but I still have to dust this staircase."

"Let that go for now," said George. "Stay here and assist Mrs. Dugan. After the family comes down, you can go upstairs and do the work there. But, don't dawdle when you do. Make sure you finish before any of them return to their bedrooms."

George picked up a tray loaded with dishes and silverware and headed for the back parlor. He closed the hall door behind him.

"Don't just sit there, girl," Mrs. Dugan growled. "Come clear out the bake oven. It's plenty hot now."

Doing as she was told, Matty carefully stepped to the far side of the fireplace and began shoveling hot ashes out of the brick oven and tossing them at the base of the main fire. She then took a dampened broom and swept the oven clear of remaining ash. All the while, she was mentally bracing herself, wondering when Mrs. Dugan would finally begin making unpleasant remarks, ones that would reveal Lydia's betrayal.

But the woman said nothing. She merely stepped past Matty, placed several small flat rounds of dough on the hot bricks and set an iron door in place.

"Now," Mrs. Dugan demanded, "go fill up my hot water cauldron. And, you make sure you keep an eye on it, keep it well-filled all day. This household uses a lot of hot water. We keep things clean. No doubt a lot more than people do where *you* live," she sneered.

Matty couldn't help feeling the sting of that, but she wasn't going to show it. Gritting her teeth, she grabbed the rope handles of two buckets and headed for the well in the back yard.

Venting her anger on the pump handle, she vigorously worked it up and down. Come the day I finish working in this house, she silently promised herself, I'm going to give that mean woman an earful!

Calming down a bit, she continued to ponder the situation. Maybe I've been worrying needlessly. Maybe Lydia didn't tell anyone about my stories. Certainly, Tilly didn't mention that when I took up her breakfast tray. Of course I only stayed a minute.

Returning to the kitchen, Matty continued doing the cook's bidding for a while until she heard the Bainbridges come down and go into the back parlor. Then, collecting some cleaning rags, an empty slop bucket and a pail of water, she hurried up the back stairs.

Beginning with Mr. Bainbridge's room, she pulled the bed covers down to the foot of the bed to give them an airing. Smoothing out the sheet and plumping up the pillows, she then turned her attention to the washstand. That involved emptying the basin into the slop bucket, drying it; then cleaning the shaving mug and brush and, finally, filling the large water pitcher with fresh water. Next, she emptied the chamber pot. Rinsing and drying it, she replaced it in its elegant chair and closed the upholstered lid. Lastly, she remade the bed and then stepped back to inspect her work. As she did so the thought came: wouldn't my Papa just love a room like this.

Gathering up her things, she closed the door and headed across the hall to Mrs. Bainbridges' room. Upon opening that door, she stopped in astonishment.

"My goodness," she whispered, "it's like a cloth garden in here! I've never seen so much embroidery."

It did seem as if the room was blooming. Most everything — bed hangings, coverlet, chair seats, table, dresser and numerous wall plaques – was adorned with colorful, flowery embroidery. Near one window, beyond the huge bed, stood a comfortable chair and sewing table. Beside it were two baskets overflowing with fabrics and yarn. Waiting in front the chair was a hoop stand holding the latest project.

"If this were Gramma's room," Matty giggled, "she'd certainly banish all that fancy stuff."

Realizing she must hurry along, she rapidly followed the same routine in returning the room to proper order. It took a bit longer than Mr. Bainbridge's room because of all the cat hair that littered part of the bedcover and several cushions. Then, quietly closing the door behind her, she went down the hall and into Lydia's room.

Unlike the other bedrooms, this was a cluttered mess. Clothing was casually tossed on furniture or floor and the scatter rugs were rumpled and askew. The floor around the washstand was wet and foot-marked. Over in the corner, the little writing desk was littered with papers and various books. Around the edges of its polished surface, Matty noticed ink stains and some scratches. If this were my room, she thought, I'd never treat it so carelessly.

Setting to work, she pictured herself enjoying such a room, the wonderful space — and the privacy. Each fine garment that she folded and put away in a dresser or hung on wooden pegs was treated as if it were her own.

Approaching the desk, Matty forced herself not to intrude on its clutter, but she couldn't help feeling envious. At home, her 'desk' was the kitchen table. What writing materials she had were neatly kept in a little basket under her bed.

Once the room was in order, Matty carried the buckets and other cleaning things into the hall and placed them near the back stairs. Returning to Lydia's door, she was about to close it when she suddenly burst into tears.

"I'll never have a room like this, not ever," she quietly sobbed. "I'll always be on the outside looking in."

Just then, the sound of a woman's voice downstairs in the front hall caused Matty to quickly collect herself.

"I don't want any argument, Lydia," the voice said. "You go into the parlor and practice your pianoforte for no less than one hour. I expect you to give a proper performance at your birthday party."

"Yes, Mama," came Lydia's reply from a distance.

Not waiting to hear more, Matty closed Lydia's door and hastily carried her buckets and other things down the back staircase.

Later that morning, Matty was sent to the storeroom on the third floor. As she reached the top of the stairs, she tried to hurry past Tilly's open doorway, hoping the woman wouldn't see her. But that was not to be.

"Come back here, you," called Tilly in her shrill voice. "I've been waiting all morning for you to tend to my room."

Matty turned back, but stayed out in the hall. Quietly she said, "I can tend to your room after I finish fluffing the feather beds in the storeroom."

"They can wait," Tilly argued. "I'm tired of your neglect!"

Keeping her composure, Matty moved on. "I'm just following George's orders," she called out as she reached the storeroom door. Slipping inside, she gratefully closed it.

In the hot, stuffy room, dust motes danced in shafts of sunlight from two small windows. Matty was pleased to find that two days' heat had done its work on the featherbeds. Kneeling on the floor beside one of them, she began the process of redistributing the feathers within, patting and pushing lumps of them, working them evenly back through sections of the cloth casing. A few minutes later, the store room door opened.

"Oh, Matty, I'm so glad to see you again," said Lydia, closing the door. She came to the edge of the bedding and seated herself on the floor. Withdrawing half a current bun from her pocket, she held it toward Matty.

"Want some?" she offered, ready to break off a piece.

"No thank you, Miss. I must keep on with my work." Matty spoke without looking up. She wished the girl would go just away.

"Won't you please call me by my name?" Lydia asked gently.

"That wouldn't be proper," replied Matty, glancing up from her work. In spite of her gloomy mood, she couldn't help responding to Lydia's pleasant smile. She returned it with one of her own.

"It's all right to call me that when we're alone," said Lydia, putting the current bun back in her pocket. Apparently having changed her mind about eating it just then, she began patting some featherbed lumps in a half-hearted way.

"You know, Matty, I hardly slept a wink since you were here. I kept thinking and thinking about what you told me, about what your family has suffered. I had no idea about such things."

Matty paused to give Lydia a questioning look. She doubted that was true.

"Oh, yes,' Lydia went right on, as if reading Matty's mind, "I have read about slavery in Papa's newspapers and magazines. But, all of that didn't seem real. I didn't *feel* anything. And, I've never been around people like you, before."

Matty said nothing as she crawled to another end of the bedding to continue the feather plumping, but Lydia remained in the same spot. It seemed obvious she didn't really want to join in the work.

"You know," said Lydia, "the subject of Negro people is a strange one for my parents. There seems to be some mystery about it. Papa is reluctant to answer my questions, which is really odd. He'll answer most anything else I ask about. And Mama, she has a fit if Negro people are even mentioned! Now she's barely speaking to Papa 'cause he let me talk him into hiring you."

Matty felt her temper rise, but managed to keep silent. I don't know why she's telling me all that stuff, she thought. But I'm not going to let her trap me into saying something I shouldn't.

"Oh, dear," Lydia suddenly said, "what did you do to your arm?"

"Your cat scratched me."

"Oh, I'm so sorry. Winston is such an unpleasant creature, but he's certainly not *my* cat. Mama's the only human he cares about. Does it hurt very much?" Lydia looked worried.

"No. Not much." Matty stood up and folded the completed feather bed. Placing a second one on the floor, she knelt back down to work on it.

"Matty, you seem different, today," said Lydia. "Are you upset about something?"

"No, I'm just trying to get on with my work."

"I'd dearly love it, if you would tell me more about your family," Lydia said quietly, "finish your story about what happened to them."

"Oh, I talk too much," replied Matty. "I really shouldn't have told you about all that."

"Why not? I want to know," said Lydia. "That's so interesting,"

Matty didn't reply.

"Is it because you don't trust me?" asked Lydia. "Truly, Matty, I wouldn't tell anyone about our conversations. And besides, there isn't anyone I'd want to share them with. Oh maybe Papa, but I wouldn't unless you approved."

She does sound sincere, thought Matty. Maybe I've misjudged her. But it's probably better if we talk about something else.

"You must be getting excited about your birthday party on Saturday," she finally said.

"I suppose." Lydia showed little enthusiasm. "This year it seems to be mostly Mama's party. She's deciding everything. And, inviting all the *right* people — most of whom I've never met."

"What about your friends?" Matty asked at she looked up.

Lydia glanced away. "I don't really have any, at least not ones who are bosom companions. Do you?"

"Well, I have lots of friends in the neighborhood," replied Matty, "ones to speak to but, I guess there's no one I'm really close to."

"What about a beau?" Lydia asked.

Matty smiled and shook her head no.

"Same for me," said Lydia. "though if Mama has her way, I'll likely be introduced to a prospective one or two this Saturday." Picking up a loose feather, she blew it into the air.

"I like the looks of some young men," she continued shyly, "but I can't imagine being married to one, at least not for years to come. I want to do something important with my life – travel, see the world and write wonderful stories. I certainly don't want to be like Mama with nothing to do, embroidering my life away."

Matty couldn't help smiling at the reference to Mrs. Bainbridge's needle work. That's exactly what she'd thought when she saw the woman's room. What a waste of life.

"It seems we think alike on many things," Matty ventured, "marriage, writing…"

"Writing?" Lydia pounced on that.

"Yes," said Matty. "I did a lot of writing in school, even some poems. I miss school. Wish they didn't make us stop at age fourteen."

"Oh, you're lucky," responded Lydia. "I don't know when I'll be finished with schooling. I'm so tired of those tutors coming to the house. And, all they teach are useless things — drawing, dancing, French."

Suddenly, there came a pounding noise on the wall. "That's Tilly," said Matty. "She's getting cross. I better hurry along."

"Oh, never mind about her," said Lydia. "She can wait. I came up to hear the rest of your story, about that time when your family was afraid some of them would be taken away and sold."

Uncertain how to answer, Matty continued pushing feathers around and making sure to force the sharp ends of the popped ones back under the fabric. I don't know, she thought. I suppose it wouldn't do any harm to tell her at least some of the rest of the story.

Chapter Ten

While plumping the last of the feather beds, Matty resumed telling Lydia about her ancestors in Portsmouth. Knowing she must hurry along, she avoided getting into a lot of detail.

"When that first slave master, Captain McIntire, died in 1768," she said, "his will left almost all his property — including my ancestors — to his nephew, Joshua Warren. Before the estate was settled and Mr. Warren moved into the house, my great grandfather, Jube, secretly started talking about escaping. He was afraid the new master would sell some of his family away. But his wife Taba talked him out of that. She was terrified they'd be caught and punished."

"Oh, my," murmured Lydia, "I can't imagine having to live like that."

"It must have been truly awful," Matty agreed. "I'm glad I didn't live then. Things were a bit different by the time I was born. I never knew I was a slave until I was five years old. That's when we got our freedom documents. Years later my grandmother told me the full story of what the family suffered.

"Anyway," she continued, "Mr. Warren, didn't sell anyone. In fact, he brought another slave with him, a handsome young man named Pompi. And, not long after that, Pompi married Bess – my grandmother. Later, near the time of the Revolution, they had Peter – my father. And, when he grew up, he married Matilda and they had me. I'm named after her.

"Then, after we got our freedom, Papa went away to find a job and a place for us to live. It took him a long while, but that job turned out to be in Boston. So, five years ago, we moved here."

Pleased with herself at having summed up the story so rapidly, Matty went back to feather-plumping.

"But surely —," Lydia said with a frown, "there must be more to tell, more to your story than that."

"Well, there is, but I'm not sure we have enough time now."

"Oh, you could tell me just a little more," Lydia insisted. "What happened in your grandparents' lives? Did the Revolution affect them at all?"

Matty stopped to think. I suppose I could tell her about the petition, that wouldn't take long.

"There was something that had an important effect on their lives," she began. "It happened about three years after the war started. My grandfather, Pompi and other black men in Portsmouth were paying close attention to what was going on. They knew what the Declaration of Independence said – that *all* men were created equal. So one night, my grandfather met with a group of his friends and they wrote up a petition for their freedom. Then they sent it to the New Hampshire Assembly.

"But, the government just ignored the petition. When my grandfather finally found out about that, he was so angry. He decided he'd use another way to try getting freedom for him and his family. Late one night, he packed some food and clothing and told my grandmother he was leaving town. He planned to find a job and somehow earn enough money to buy their freedom. She begged to go with him, but he said it would be safer if she and Peter stayed behind to wait for his return. But then, he never did come back."

"What happened to him?" Lydia asked.

"No one knows. Gramma Bess said he might have been captured and sold to a plantation owner in the South…or maybe he just died."

Matty fell silent, hoping that the girl's curiosity was satisfied.

"There's something else you haven't told me about," Lydia spoke up. "You haven't told me why your father chose the name 'Smith' for your family."

"Oh, that's right," Matty said. "Well, Papa didn't want us to be known by that slave name 'Warren', the one written on our freedom documents. And, since he is a smith, a blacksmith, the choice seemed right. Now he only goes by the name 'Smith', but Gramma Bess insists that the rest of us should keep the other name, too. She worries there might be some legal trouble if we don't."

Having finished the second featherbed, Matty stood up and smoothed down her skirts. "So," she said, smiling at Lydia, "that's why I'm called Matty Warren Smith."

Those words were hardly out of her mouth when pounding on the wall began again, along with insistent ringing of a little bell.

"That Tilly!" said Lydia in disgust. "I'm going to tell her to stop her noise."

"Oh please, Lydia, don't say anything. That might cause trouble for me. Besides, I'm all finished here. I can attend to her needs now."

"All right, I won't," Lydia agreed. "But I hope you and I can talk soon again. There's so much more I want to know."

During the rest of that day there were no more lengthy encounters between the girls. Demands of the cook, an irritable Tilly and a busy household kept Matty constantly on the go, hurrying from one task to the next.

By mid afternoon, the house finally grew quiet. Lydia and her mother had retired to their rooms for a nap. Mr. Bainbridge was in his library and George was away on errands. Even Mrs. Dugan had nodded off in a rocking chair located well beyond the ever-hot fireplace. As for Matty, her chance for a rest of sorts was taking place on the back steps while dealing with several freshly-killed chickens.

Thank goodness for shade on this side of the house, she thought. Relaxing into a familiar task, she dipped a chicken into a pot of hot water, withdrew it after a minute or so and then began pulling out handfuls of loosened feathers. It was a messy job, but one she didn't really mind. Determined not to let the cook find fault, she took special care to remove every bit of leftover pin feathers.

This must be my 'feather' day, she thought with a grin. Then her mind took a more serious direction, thinking about her earlier encounter with Lydia. You know, she told herself, I don't think I did any harm at all by answering her questions, telling her more about our family.

In fact, I think I did something good, something useful. If what she told me is true, then she really is beginning to understand about our peoples' suffering, at least more than she did before.

Maybe, that's what we should be doing…finding ways to tell more white people the personal stories about us. Help them see how truly dreadful slavery is. And, the risks our people took to get free of it. And, are still taking, she reminded herself. If only we could make white folks understand about all that, then maybe their hatred would go away.

Warming to the idea, Matty began daydreaming of what she might do in such an effort. I could begin by writing down my family's story, she thought, get Gramma Bess to give me more details, make it a really good story. Then I could talk to other people and write down their stories. And then, someday I might find a way to get all the stories put into a book for the whole country to read.

Oh, you silly girl, her inner voice taunted. *What an impossible idea! A book would cost a lot of money. You'd never have enough to do that. Even so, you might never find a printer willing to do a girl's – a black girl's book.*

Well, she silently argued, I don't think it's impossible. That poet we read about in school — Phillis Wheatley — she got her writing printed.

Excited about her project, Matty quickly grabbed the next chicken by the legs. Dunking it in and then out of hot water she attacked its feathers with renewed vigor.

Soon as I get home tonight, I'm going to start writing. I don't care if the candlelight does bring in the bugs. I won't let that stop me.

Chapter Eleven

*T*he rest of that week seemed to speed by in a pur-
poseful whirl for Matty, both at work and at home. Despite
Bess's mild objections but, with her father and great uncle's
encouragement, Matty had begun her writing project. Ned
even supplied her with extra paper. For half a penny, he
bought several discarded account books. Cutting out unused
pages, he bound them neatly together with yarn to make a
booklet.

By Friday, however, Matty was beginning to realize
that her project would take a long time, especially at the rate
she was going. She had only written a page and half and both
of those were marred with numerous crossed out words and
even whole lines. At the start, she thought writing her family's story would be as easy as the telling had been. But putting
pen to paper was different. It seemed to bring forth another
person in her head, one eager to criticize and cause self-doubt.

Up on Beacon Hill during that week, serious preparations got under way, not only for Lydia's birthday party, but for
a host of relatives coming for Boston's July Fourth celebration.

Caught up in such a flurry of activity, Matty seldom
encountered Lydia. Apparently, the girl was being kept busy,
ensnared in her mother's preparations and shopping trips.

When the girls did meet, Matty would venture a smile
or a wave. Lydia, however, kept insisting on a bit more. Hastily
she'd whisper a question such as, "What's your favorite
flower?"

"Wild roses," Matty would whisper before hurrying on.

Another time it was, "What's your favorite food?"

"Gramma Bess's ginger cake."

When she could take the time, Matty joined Lydia's game with questions of her own. On one occasion, she asked, "What kind of books do you like to read?"

"Novels and poetry," Lydia replied. "What about you?"

"I like Greek mythology best," said Matty.

It was a fun, if hasty way, to get to know one another and Matty felt warmed by it.

On Tuesday morning, window washers came and all the Bainbridges drove off in their carriage for the day. Matty followed the workmen from room to room, clearing the way, then setting things back in place. After that, in addition to her regular duties, there was brass polishing – a bigger and more tedious job than she could have imagined. By the end of the day, her forearms ached from rubbing and polishing a host of brass candle holders and ornaments for ten fireplaces. The caustic polish solution left her hands cracked and sore.

On Wednesday and Thursday, Matty gave the guest rooms on the second and third floors a thorough cleaning. Then, on Friday, major food and party preparations got under way. And with that, Matty became aware of an unpleasant change in the atmosphere.

Tension and shortness of temper invaded the household, upstairs and down. Even George abandoned his gentle ways and issued orders with a snap. Often, these were followed by references to Mrs. Bainbridge's exacting requirements for 'perfect' hospitality and entertainments.

Matty was amazed by the variety and lavishness of foods being prepared. There was even a French confectioner who had been brought in to practice his art. However, she couldn't help noticing the contrast between this household and her own happier home. Never, would her family have approached a party or celebration with such an unpleasant, joyless spirit.

At 6 a.m. on Saturday, July fourth, Matty was in the process of filling Mrs. Dugan's water barrel when bells began ringing all over Boston. Hastily, she took empty buckets and returned to the backyard pump so she could revel in the joyous sounds. By official decree, steeple bells would ring forth for one hour in honor of American Independence.

"Isn't that a wonderful way to celebrate my birthday," Lydia called down from her bedroom window.

"Good morning, Miss," Matty called back as she began working the pump handle, "and happy birthday."

"Thank you," Lydia replied. "Just wish they'd do that ringing at a sensible hour so I could sleep. This is going to be a long day for me." She yawned and stretched, before turning away from the window.

Going to be a long one for me, too, Matty thought with some resentment.

And, that day did prove a long and trying one for Matty. With a house full of company, she was kept scurrying upstairs and down, trying to supply their needs. Most visitors treated her with disdainful silence. One woman, however, looked right at her and said to another, "What's a Negro doing in this house? I didn't think Mrs. Bainbridge would allow one of them here!"

Ignoring that as best she could, Matty kept reminding herself, I'll only have to put up with such nastiness for another week. Then I'll find a job elsewhere. Surely, there must be places I can go where black people are treated more kindly.

Around nine o'clock, the Bainbridges and their visitors trooped off in their finest attire for the start of celebrations in front of the State house on Beacon Street. Upstairs, in the second floor hallway, Matty breathed a sigh of relief when she heard the front door close. Now, she thought, maybe I'll get a moment to cool my toes. Putting aside her cleaning things, she slipped off her shoes and settled down on the top step of the back stairs.

Thinking about the exciting events up on the hill, she wished she could be there and hear the patriotic speeches and then see the grand military parade and cannon salute on the Common. But she knew people of color wouldn't be welcome. Maybe, she thought, some of our black veterans of the Revolutionary War will attend. Even so, I suspect they'll be kept on the edges of the crowd.

Disliking the bitter taste of resentment, she tried to put it aside and simply enjoy the quiet of the house above the bustling kitchen. Her enjoyment, however, was soon interrupted when George appeared at the bottom of the stairs.

"Matty, he called out crossly, "there's no time for that! You scurry along and finish getting the bedrooms in order. Then come back down here. We don't have a moment to waste."

A little past two, before party guests began arriving, it was Lydia who provided Matty with a welcome break. Barging into the kitchen, the elegantly dressed birthday girl insisted

Matty leave her pot scrubbing to view the dining room scene. Ignoring Mrs. Dugan's grumbled objections and George's frown, Lydia led Matty into the hallway, closed the kitchen door and then opened the back entrance to the dining room.

Matty drew in her breath, amazed at the sight before her. The dining table had been extended part way into the front parlor. Its long surface gleamed with fine white linen, bright silverware, delicately etched glassware and lovely china in a blue and white design. At each of twenty-two place settings was a snow white napkin folded like a little boat under sail. On every dinner plate was a round, golden brown sugar wafer embossed with the Great Seal of the United States. In the center of the table, amidst a ring of red, white and blue flowers, was a large stemmed glass plate holding a tall paper cone covered with strawberries. A stiff coating of glistening sugar held them all firmly in place. Around the base of the cone were grape leaves holding small pink flowers made of spun sugar. The rest of the table was filled with platters of various meats, bowls of summer vegetables and savory meat pies.

On the bow-front sideboard was an impressive array of decorated cakes, large and small, glasses of colored jellies and other desserts.

Matty was just about to make a comment when Mrs. Bainbridge entered the front parlor. Unaware of the girls, the woman immediately turned to face a gilt-framed oval mirror hanging between the front windows. Holding their silence, the girls watched as the woman inspected her hairdo and then adjusted the cap sleeves of her gauzy white cotton gown. For Matty, this was the first time she'd actually seen, rather than heard Mrs. Bainbridge.

Suddenly, the woman scowled as the mirror revealed the girls standing behind her at the far end of the dining room. Without turning, she cried out, "Lydia, you get that Negra out of my sight! Put her in the cellar until this party's over!"

Too astonished to move, Matty looked at Lydia, hoping she'd intervene, but the girl stood silent. Disappointed and angry, Matty fled out into the back hallway, nearly colliding with George as he was heading toward the kitchen.

"Steady there, girl," he said, as he moved back. Apparently, he'd heard Mrs. Bainbridge's outburst for he gave Matty a knowing look before ushered her into the kitchen. With his back to the closed door, he said quietly, "I know that wasn't your fault, but you better do what Mrs. B. wants. Try not to fret about it. Just go down cellar and keep yourself busy while you're there. Sort through the potato barrel to check for any rotten ones. Then, after you've finished that, look about for dusting and sweeping. When it's time for dishwashing I'll call you to come up."

As Matty descended the steep stairs into the gloom of the cellar, all she could think about was Lydia's silence. Why didn't she speak up, explain things to her mother? Oh, how could I ever have thought she was my friend!

Chapter Twelve

*O*n her way home that night, Matty angrily muttered, "I don't care. I'm *not* going back there! No! Never!" Her distress and the gathering darkness dulled her sight as she reached the bottom of the hill and rounded the corner onto Cambridge Street.

"Look out for my ladder," a man hollered.

"Oh, I'm sorry. Excuse me." Matty carefully stepped around a short ladder leaning against the brick wall of a used clothing store and barbershop. Near the top rung, a lamplighter was attending to a large four-sided glass lantern suspended from curved iron brackets. Suddenly, the whale-oil-fed wick flamed up to cast a dim pool of light at Matty's feet. Moving on, she was grateful to see other pools of light ahead, lanterns marking alleyways and street corners.

Beneath some of those lanterns, a few people stood talking and laughing, enjoying this Fourth of July night. Such scenes did nothing to lighten Matty's heart. She was still feeling the hurt, still reliving her day and the bitter injustice of Mrs. Bainbridge's treatment — as well as the misery of spending hours in the cellar, while partygoers' merriment sounded overhead.

Sitting down there, she had covered her face with her apron and let the tears flow. After a while, she half-heartedly followed George's instructions and sorted through a great barrel of potatoes. When the first rotten potato came to light she held it gingerly between two fingers. Hesitating only a moment, she threw it, worms and all, against the low ceiling.

It felt so good to vent her anger. Twice more, she did the same thing. Then, feeling foolish about the mess she had made, she hastened to clean it up before anyone came into the cellar.

Nearly three hours passed before George finally called her back upstairs. Awaiting her was a mountain of dirty dishes and Mrs. Dugan's smug, hate-filled stare. Matty was sorely tempted to head for the back door and leave, but she resisted the urge. I won't give that woman the satisfaction of seeing me quit, she thought. Holding her head high, she walked over to the sink.

With no one offering to help her, it took Matty a long time to finish her task. But when it was done, the last dish dried and put away and the last iron cooking pot set by the fireplace to dry, Matty hurried out the back door without speaking to anyone. Unfortunately, it wasn't until she was nearly home that she realized she'd forgotten to ask George for her week's wages.

Now, reaching home, Matty found Bess sitting alone at the kitchen table reading their well-worn Bible. Beside it, a candle cast flickering light on the pages while tempting fluttering moths toward certain disaster. Matty slumped down on the bench across the table from her grandmother. She put her head down on her arms.

"They shouldn't have kept you so late," Bess said, looking over her spectacles at Matty. "It's worrisome, you being out there alone after dark."

"It was that awful mountain of dishes from the party," Matty responded, looking up with tear-filled eyes. "Oh, Gramma, I can't go back there anymore. It's *so* dreadful."

Reaching across the table, Bess patted the girl's arm. "Let me get you a drink of water. Then you can tell me all about it."

Annoyed with herself for giving in to tears, Matty grabbed the hem of her apron and wiped them away. Composing herself, she looked around the room. "Guess the folks upstairs have gone to bed," she commented. "But where's Papa and Uncle Ned? They're not out celebrating, are they?"

"Of course not," said Bess. "You know better than that! We don't celebrate the Fourth of July. That war certainly was not about *our* freedom!"

Returning to the table with a filled mug, she sat down beside her granddaughter. "Your papa and Ned went to a committee meeting," she said. "It seems there's some problem with the town over the parade route for our celebration on the fourteenth. I expect they'll be back any minute.

"As for the boarders," she continued, "there's just Annie and the little ones upstairs. Heaven knows where Sam and the others are. I just hope they come home at a sensible hour… or at least not awaken us whenever they do." Waving aside some circling moths, Bess moved the mug closer to Matty. "Have some of that, child. Then tell me exactly what happened today."

I'm not a *child*, Matty thought, gritting her teeth. And to prove that, she straightened up, determined to relate the day's events in a grownup dispassionate way. Taking a sip of the water, she began her reply as if it were simply a story, something interesting that might have happened to someone else. Pleased with this approach, she took the time to give her grandmother a detailed picture of food preparations, the appearance and attitudes of some of the Bainbridge visitors she had encountered. Then she described the amazing dining room display. But when the moment came to bring Mrs. Bainbridge into the telling, Matty lost control. The rest of her story came forth amid tears and snuffles.

"I don't understand why that woman hates me so. I did nothing to deserve that. And, Lydia — I thought she was my friend — but she just stood there and didn't say anything to help me!"

"That's the way with some white folks," Bess said in disgust. She put a comforting arm around Matty's waist, drawing her close.

"Oh why," Matty burst out, "why did I have to be born black! It's so unfair!"

"Now you listen here, young lady," said Bess, drawing away and angrily pounding her fist on the table. "I won't have you saying such a thing, mocking God. You're blaming the color of our skin for white people's hatefulness. But they're in the wrong, not us!"

"No, Gramma, I didn't mean that."

"Yes, you did."

"Did what?" asked Peter, as he and Ned walked into the kitchen.

Peter leaned on the end of the table waiting for an answer while the little wall clock busily struck the hour of ten. Ned, seeming disinterested, began clearing space for their fold-down bed.

"Your daughter," Bess's voice rose in anger, "thinks white skin is better than black, thinks God made a mistake."

"Aw, Momma, don't be too hard on her," said Peter as he and his uncle picked up the bench on the opposite side of the table and moved it under the front window. "I don't believe Matty really means that. She's just going through something we've all been through," he said. "It's hard sometimes, not to begin blaming yourself when all you get from white folks is meanness."

Bewildered by her grandmother's anger and her father's words, Matty kept silent.

"Sister," Ned spoke up, "you oughtn't to heap your anger on Matty. You know she's not to blame. You're angry at what those white folks have done — making her doubt herself, feel inferior. But you shouldn't take it out on her."

While he was speaking he had come around the table and now he put a comforting hand on Matty's shoulder. "You know, my girl," he said, "you're now dealing with what I call the black folks' second struggle — the struggle that comes after we get free of slavery.

"We've managed to get our bodies free, but for some of us there's still that struggle to get our minds free, free of the white man's rule. You're luckier than many folks, Matty, 'cause you were so young when we got our freedom. You never really knew what it was like to be treated like a piece of property, constantly reminded that white people consider us inferior beings."

"I'm sure getting that now," Matty muttered.

"Yes, you are," agreed Ned. "But you've got to fight against that as best you can. I know it's not easy because you'd lose your job if you spoke your mind. But don't you ever let their hatred cause you to turn upon yourself. You've got to be a good friend to yourself. Your self respect is the most precious thing you'll ever have."

For a moment or so, no one said anything. Then Peter broke the stillness. "You'd make a fine preacher, Uncle Ned," he said with a smile.

"Well, I could have told her the same thing if I'd gotten the chance," said Bess in annoyance as she got up from the bench. "But," she added with a sigh, "brother Ned is right. There is a lot of anger boiling around in us grown-ups because of what we've been through. But we mustn't take it out on each other."

Assuming her usual role of being in charge, Bess indicated it was time for bed by hugging first her son and then Ned. Lighting a second candle from the one on the table, she waited while Matty also bid her father and uncle goodnight.

Upon entering their bedroom, Matty quietly said, "I am sorry I upset you, Gramma."

Nodding her acceptance of that, Bess set the candleholder on the bedside table. Then she opened their window a bit wider and quickly pinched the candle's wick with fingertips. "We'll undress in the dark," she murmured. "No sense bringing in more bugs."

"Wish I'd been able to get home earlier," said Matty, as she lay down on the bed. "I'd like to have done some more writing."

"You know," Bess spoke up, "I guess it is useful that you're writing down some of our family stories. But, that should only be for your children and grandchildren someday. Thinking you might get it printed up as a book is such an impossible idea."

Matty set her jaw and made no reply. Gramma doesn't understand what I'm trying to do, she thought, but I'm not going to let her discourage me.

"I'm wondering," Bess spoke out again, "as unpleasant as it is at the Bainbridges, I think you might consider staying on. It'll only be for another week or so. That way, you could get a reference to help you find another job."

"I wouldn't get a reference, not with the way Mrs. Bainbridge acted."

"But from what you've told us, it's the Mister who's in charge and he hasn't found any fault with you, has he?"

"No, but I don't want to go back there anymore. Trouble is, I forgot to ask George for my wages before I left." Matty paused to think. "Maybe," she finally said, "I could go back on Monday, do some work as if I was going to stay, then get the wages and leave right after that."

"I don't think that's a good idea," said Bess, "but you sleep on it and let your mind come clear. Goodnight."

Bracing herself, Matty expected to hear that annoying word 'child' come forth. When it didn't, she smiled.

"Gramma," she said in a sleepy voice, "earlier tonight you called me 'young lady'. I really like hearing that."

Chapter Thirteen

*O*n Monday, Matty did go back to work. But, that day did not proceed as she had planned. Arriving at the Bainbridges' back gate, she gathered an armload of firewood as usual and entered the kitchen. To her surprise, at that early hour, Mrs. Dugan and George were already in a flurry of activity preparing to serve breakfast.

"Don't stand there with your mouth gapping, girl," Mrs. Dugan growled. "Dump the wood and then fill up the water cauldron. We're running low on hot water and guests are wanting a washup."

"Yes, do hurry along," George told her more gently. "Some of the guests are already up and dressing. They hope to catch an early stagecoach out of town."

During the next hour or so, she followed her familiar routine, working about the kitchen, seeing to Tilly's needs and carrying hot water upstairs for visitors and family members — other than Mrs. Bainbridge. George attended to her requirements.

Finally, after Matty had made numerous trips upstairs and down, George gave her new instructions. "Put aside your other work," he said. "Get some cleaning cloths and come with me to the library. Mr. Bainbridge has ordered that you spend the morning dusting his books."

"But, I need to talk to you about my wages from last week."

"Never mind that," George replied. "You'll get your wages at the end of the day." He opened the hallway door and looked around as if making sure no one was about, then he signaled Matty to follow him.

"This is a big responsibility," he said as they entered the library, "and I want you to take your time and do it properly. Remove each book, carefully dust it and lay it aside. Remember to keep them in the same order in which they came off the shelf. When you have dusted the empty shelf, replace the books in the proper order. Some of the volumes are very old and valuable so handle them with care. And, you are not to leave here until I come for you. Mr. Bainbridge thinks it's best if you keep out of the way today." With that said, George left the room and quietly closed the door.

Looking around at hundreds of books awaiting her attention, Matty couldn't help smiling. "What a treasure room," she whispered, "and I have it all to myself."

Letting her eyes roam over a nearby shelf, she spotted one or two familiar books, ones she had read at school or among their small, second-hand collection at home. Gently, she trailed her fingers over fine leather-bound editions of *Whitcomb's Poems, Aesop's Fables, Robinson Crusoe, Whittington and His Cat.* Looking further, she soon moved past that limited, light reading section. The rest of the room reflected Professor Bainbridge's scholarly interests.

Smiling, she whispered, "I dearly wish George would forget to come back for me."

Going to the lowest shelf behind Mr. Bainbridges' desk, Matty sat on the floor and pulled out a heavy, oversized world atlas. She dusted its spine and covers and, hesitating only a moment, she opened it. I'll just peek at a few pages, she told herself.

Absorbed in her travel about the world, Matty didn't hear the library door open and close. "Where are you, Matty?" Lydia called out.

Startled, Matty hastily closed the book and stood up. "I'm here, doing my dusting."

"Oh, I'm so glad you came back," said Lydia. "I was afraid that, after what happened, you wouldn't. Mamma was terribly wrong to treat you like that."

Well, why didn't you come to my defense, Matty wanted to shout. But didn't. Suppressing her anger, she sat back down. I won't let her see that I care, she thought while pulling out the next oversized book. Maybe if I ignore her, she'll just go away.

"Matty, I have so much to tell you," Lydia chattered on as she came around the desk and knelt down on the floor. "Things that explain about Mamma's attitude, things Papa told me."

Despite her intent to keep her distance, Matty looked up. "What things?" she asked.

"Well, you see, it was awfully hot last night," said Lydia, "and I couldn't get to sleep. So I came down here for a book and found Papa. He started talking about what happened to you on Saturday and he explained why Mama gets so upset about Negro people. And, he talked about a lot of others things, too." Not waiting for Matty's reaction, Lydia launched into a full accounting of that late night chat.

The hall clock had just finished striking midnight when Lydia entered the library to find her father seated at his desk.

"Excuse me, Papa," she whispered. "I'm sorry to disturb you."

"Oh, that's all right," he said. "Guess I'm not the only one who can't sleep. Come on in and sit down a few minutes. There's something I've been meaning to speak to you about."

Wide-eyed with interest, Lydia put her candle holder down on a small table and settled into her favorite seat, that roomy old green wing chair.

Her father looked at her thoughtfully. "I feel badly about what happened to young Matty," he said. "I blame myself for that, for agreeing to hire her in the first place."

"But Papa, I don't understand why Mamma acts the way she does, why she's always so angry about Negro people."

"It's got to do with her father's death a long time ago," he replied. "Every time Amelia sees black people or hears something about them, it reminds her of that. And, she won't let go of the past. I know it's wrong and I've tried to help her, but it's useless."

"What happened to my grandfather Tilford? Nobody's ever told me much about him or about Mama's growing up on that North Carolina farm."

"Well, it wasn't just a farm," her father replied. "It was a big tobacco plantation and her father had more than fifty slaves. During the Revolution, when British forces came near there, the slaves heard rumors they could get their freedom if they took up with the King's men. When the slaves started running off, your grandfather went after them with a gun. He shot and killed several men and a woman. Then another slave managed to take his gun away and killed him with it. After that, your grandmother Tilford and her two daughters couldn't manage on their own so they came north to Massachusetts."

"That's terrible, Papa. Poor Mama — and poor everyone else, too." Lydia stared at the glowing candle for a moment. "I had no idea my grandfather was a slave owner," she said. "Why didn't you tell me about this before?"

"I didn't think it was anything you needed to know. But I guess now you do." He looked searchingly at his daughter's face and then added, "I suppose while I'm at it, I might as well tell you the rest, about my own family's involvement in all that."

"Your family owned slaves?" Lydia asked in wonder.

"Not so much owning, as buying and selling them," he confessed.

"It was a shameful business, but father kept my brother and me from knowing much about it until we were older. He sent us away to school in England. When we finally came home to Boston, I wanted nothing to do with the slave trade, but my brother was eager for the money. He soon took over management of father's ships. He used to laugh at my disgust with dealing in slaves, telling me it was just an old family business, one they'd been in for more than a hundred years. I hated knowing that."

Though shocked at what she was hearing, Lydia was curious to know more. "Papa, when did your family get into the slave trade?"

"I don't know exactly, he replied. "Likely, my great, great grandfather got into it around 1671. That's when his first ship was launched in Boston. Like other merchants, he shipped lumber and dried cod to the Caribbean plantations and sometimes bought a few slaves to sell in New England. Later on, his ships went to Africa and got involved in supplying slaves to the West Indies and various colonies, north as well as south."

"So now, Matty, you understand," said Lydia, looking pleased with herself. "Mamma can't help the way she acts."

Matty thoughts whirled angrily, but she remained silent. *What's she expect me to say? Am I supposed to just accept that, think that makes everything all right?* Finally, she looked at Lydia and said, "I think it was sad what happened to your mama, but that's really no excuse for her to hate all black people. And, after all, your grandfather did kill three innocent people just because they were trying to get their freedom." Seeing a look of surprise on Lydia's face, she added, "Well, it doesn't matter what I think. I won't be working here after today."

"Oh no, we need you here, at least until Tilly gets back on her feet." Lydia reached out and touched Matty's arm. "I wish you could stay even after that."

Matty moved away to finish re-shelving a group of books on rare plants and birds. *She must think I'm stupid,* she thought. *Why would I stay here and continue to be mistreated!* Bringing more dusty books to the desk, she glanced at Lydia's earnest, friendly face. In spite of herself, Matty felt her anger fade.

"I can't imagine your mother would allow me to stay," she said quietly. "And, even if she did, I'd still have to put up with all those nasty remarks from Mrs. Dugan and Tilly."

"Oh, don't worry about Momma. Papa said he would talk with her and explain again that your stay is only temporary. As for the others, I'll tell Papa what they're doing and he'll get George to give them a stern lecture."

Maybe that would help, Matty thought, but I doubt it.

Changing the subject she said, "Lydia, I've been wondering why you told me the rest of what your father said, about his family being in the slave trade?"

"Well," she replied with a shrug, "I just thought you'd be interested in that part. And, it does show that Papa's always been against slavery and doesn't feel the way Mama does about Negro people."

A knock came at the door and George entered carrying what appeared to be a bundle of mail. "Excuse me, Miss Lydia," he said, placing the bundle on the desk. Looking at Matty he frowned as if telling her to keep on with her work, but he made no comment before leaving the room.

"Goody," Lydia burst out, "maybe there's something for me."

She sorted through the bundle. "Look here, Matty, the new Boston Town Directory has come. Now I can see exactly where you live. Your father's name is —,"

"Peter Smith, on Butolph Street," Matty responded as Lydia proceeded to leaf through the booklet. The first section gave an alphabetical listing of male residents and their occupations.

"He isn't here," murmured Lydia. "Maybe he's listed in the other section, the one that lists people on a particular street."

"May I take a look," Matty asked, coming to lean over the desk. She re-checked the first section. Then she turned to the next section to look among names listed for Butolph Street. But her father's name wasn't there. "That's so strange. I don't understand why not."

Out of curiosity, she went back to the front section to look for other peoples' names, friends and members of her church. But none were listed. She began looking for them in the street name section and was astonished at what she found. Instead of their name being listed at their particular location on a street, either they weren't listed at all or the word 'Blacks' was printed.

She turned to Belknap Street where so many black families lived, either on that street or in courtyards and alley-ways behind it. But she saw no familiar names. Instead, here and there on the page the word 'Blacks' appeared. At Mays Court where the African Meeting House stood surrounded by homes of some of its members, only one black person was list-ed – the Reverend Tobias Jennings.

"This is terrible," Matty cried. "We've all been left out." She shook her head in disgust. "My Uncle Ned is so right. Boston is never going to care about black people. We'd all be better off if we did go to Africa."

Not wanting Lydia to see her angry tears, Matty turned back to the shelves and the task at hand.

Lydia kept on leafing through the directory. Suddenly she said,

"Here he is. Your father and all your people are listed at the back of the book. See, everything's all right now." She brought the booklet over for Matty to see.

Staring at a section headed 'AFRICANS', Matty's anger only grew. Everything is certainly not all right, she thought, glancing through that section. Nearly two hundred men's names were listed. The publisher, however, hadn't bothered to give anyone's occupation the way he had for white residents.

"This just proves what I said before," Matty com-plained. "Black people have no chance here. Just because of our skin color, we're treated unfairly, kept out of society, have laws made against us! Now, even that town directory isolates us from the rest of the population. It's all so mean!"

Looking surprised and uncomfortable at this further outburst, Lydia backed away and curled up in the wing chair. Silently, she watched as Matty snatched up several dust cloths and went over to an open window beyond the desk. Vigorously and repeatedly, Matty shook the cloths –more so than necessary – apparently trying to vent her anger.

Finally, Lydia spoke up. "I guess I hadn't really thought about all that, Matty. You are right. It isn't fair the way your people are treated. Something should be done. At least about that directory."

For a few moments, neither girl spoke. Then Lydia suddenly sprang up from her chair.

"I know what can be done," she said. "We should write a stern letter to the publisher, make him see how wrong that is. Or," she added brightly, "write to His Excellency the Governor. I feel sure he would set things to right."

"Oh, that is…." Matty almost said 'ridiculous', but politely modified her words. "I don't think that would change anything. Those men would just laugh at such a letter, especially one from us."

"Well, something needs to be done," Lydia insisted. "I'd really like to find a way we can protest, make people come to their senses!"

Matty made no response as she resumed the dusting. *I suppose*, she thought, *it is nice that Lydia cares, even if her idea is impossible.*

Lydia moved restlessly about the room. She looked out the window and then returned to the desk to go through the mail again. Earlier, out in the hall, there had been noises of departing guests, but now the only sounds were of clocks striking the hour of eleven. As usual, the tall one in the hall pursued its measured, steady chime while in the library a small brass mantle clock finished its task well ahead of its ponderous rival.

"Matty," Lydia finally spoke up. "Please don't leave before the end of this week. I want so much to talk more about this with you, find a way to change that directory.

"Tomorrow, I'm going away with Mama and Papa to visit relatives in Newburyport, but we'll be back on Friday. In the meantime, you and I should put on our thinking caps about a letter of some sort — to someone." Opening the library door, she paused and turned around. "Promise me you'll be here when I get back?"

Matty hesitated a moment while studying the girl's earnest expression. She felt a flicker of hope, then squelched it. There's nothing either of us can do about that directory, she thought. But, it would be nice to be in Lydia's company a little while longer. And, I'd also like getting another week's wages.

"Yes," she finally replied, "if nobody objects, I'll be here."

Chapter Fourteen

That evening, in a voice full of indignation, Matty told her family about the Boston Directory. Their response, as they sat around the kitchen table, came as a great disappointment.

"Well, that's just the way things are," said Peter, returning to his newspaper with a shrug. "No need for a fuss."

Bess made no immediate comment. She simply looked up over her spectacles with a tight-lipped expression, one that clearly conveyed her annoyance. Matty wasn't sure if it was directed at her or the topic at hand.

Only Ned had kept steady, kindly eyes on Matty's face while she spoke. When she finished, he looked down at the open Bible before him and shook his head from side to side. "Seems as though," he said, "no matter how hard ol' Joshua blows his horn, there's some walls that aren't ever coming down. They're just gettin' higher."

"Well, I see no reason for any upset," Bess scolded. "That directory merely shows we are making progress, that we are now recognized, tax-paying citizens. I feel sure that, in time, they'll change that listing and put African people in beside everyone else. You've got to learn patience, Matty. It's going to take a while to prove ourselves, get white people's respect."

"Aw, Sister," grumbled Ned, "you keep on saying the same ol' thing."

"And, you keep on telling me I'm wrong," Bess retorted.

"Gramma," Matty gently intervened, "wouldn't it be a good idea if someone wrote a letter to the publisher and let him know that at least some of us think that directory needs changing now? I have some ideas of what could be written."

"That's foolishness," Bess quickly responded. "That would not be a good idea. And, it would certainly be improper for a young girl like you to involve herself in that. You need to learn that some things are best left alone." Turning her attention to Ned, she ended further discussion. "It's getting late," she told him. "We need to get on with our Bible reading and prayers."

Disheartened by her family's reaction, Matty found it hard to concentrate during this family ritual. Instead of the warm, loving feeling it always brought, she felt only annoyance and disappointment.

How can they be so unconcerned, she wondered. We can't just accept what is. We've got to speak out to change things!

Like a shuttle on a loom, her restless mind began speeding back and forth between hopefulness and despair. Oh why bother, she thought. It's useless. When the war's over, we should leave this country. No sense staying where we aren't wanted.

Then, going the other way, she argued, no, we mustn't give up. Now that we're free, we have rights and we should be treated with respect, same as everyone else.

At one point, she scolded herself for getting upset about any of that. Maybe it is best to be patient, just go along, ignore all that unpleasantness. After all, if I hadn't gone up to the Common that day, if I had simply delivered Gramma's bread to Reverend Jennings and come back home, I'd be so much happier now. I'd never have met Lydia and those nasty, prejudiced women up there and I wouldn't know about that awful directory.

But, I did. And I do. Now I can't close my mind to that.

Next day, as Matty carried out her morning routine at the Bainbridges, she kept hoping for at least a brief encounter with Lydia. She wanted to tell her she had changed her mind about that directory. She did want to try writing a letter. But no such meeting occurred.

A little past nine o'clock, Matty watched from an upstairs window as the smartly dressed family climbed into their shiny black open carriage and was driven away. Her last sight of them, as they went down Walnut Street, was Mrs. Bainbridge's fluttering parasol and Lydia hanging onto her tall-crowned straw bonnet.

"I hope she does have her thinking cap on," Matty whispered. "I'm certainly going to put on mine for a possible letter."

During days that followed, a stifling heat wave, the first of the season, descended over Boston. Life in the crowded North Slope village became oppressive. Each morning, Matty was grateful to reach the top of Beacon Hill in order to fill her lungs with fresher, if not entirely dust-free air.

With the Bainbridges away, her workload became lighter and she was pleased to notice a slight change in the behavior of Mrs. Dugan and Tilly – at least in regard to their making nasty remarks. But, despite whatever talking-to they may have gotten from George, their tone of voice and unfriendly stares remained the same.

Fortunately, she spent most of that week alone in the library, continuing to remove dust from its abundant collections. And, all the while, that Boston Town Directory lay on the desk in plain sight. At times it seemed to taunt her, but at other moments it spurred her on, encouraging her to form sentences that might convince the publisher to see the errors of his ways.

Friday afternoon, Matty was sitting on the back steps when she heard Lydia's high voice coming from the kitchen.

"George, where is Matty? I need her to come and unpack my trunk."

"She's outside, shelling peas, Miss Lydia," George replied. "I'll send her along as soon as she finishes."

Anxious to see Lydia, Matty picked up the pace of shelling.

Within a short time, she dumped the empty pods on the trash heap at the far end of the yard and deposited a large bowl of peas on the kitchen worktable. Straightening her mob cap and brushing down her apron, she hurried up the back stairs.

"Oh, Matty, I couldn't wait to see you," said Lydia as she quietly closed her bedroom door. "I've got the most wonderful idea for you."

"I'm pleased to see you, too," responded Matty. "I've been thinking about that letter and I've even written down parts for one." She started to withdraw a slip of paper from her pocket.

"Never mind about that," Lydia said impatiently. Then, glancing at the wall which separated her room from her mother's, she lowered her voice. "I've got something much better that we can do. It's somewhat daring, but I believe it can work."

Frowning with annoyance, Matty let the paper slide back into place and walked over to a small deerskin-covered trunk near the window. Lifting its lid, she removed a cloth cover and began lifting out Lydia's garments. I worked hard on those sentences, she thought. I don't want to just throw them away.

Lydia stretched herself comfortably across the bed and began talking in a near whisper. "Well, you see, Matty, at first I was also working on that letter, but then I got to thinking. If we could get *other* people to write letters, get them upset about the directory, then that would surely force the editor to change things."

Pondering that idea, Matty brought a filmy pink summer dress over to the foot of the bed. Smoothing it out, she began folding it for storage in a chest of drawers. Then, pausing in her work, she looked up at Lydia.

"I don't know who would write such letters," she whispered. "Though maybe," she continued, "I could talk to people at our meeting house about that directory during the nooning. "That is," she grinned, "if Gramma Bess doesn't hush me up."

"I suppose you could do that," said Lydia, "but my idea is much better. You could come with me to our meeting house and talk to people there."

Matty was astonished. What in the world is she talking about? What a crazy idea. Gathering up the folded garment, she went to the chest of drawers and carefully laid it in place. Turning around, she whispered, "I could never do that, Lydia. My family would never allow such a scandalous thing."

"They wouldn't have to know about it," said Lydia, coming up to a sitting position. "You see, Matty, I've got it all planned out," she quickly continued. "This Sunday you and I will —"

"Oh, no," Matty interrupted. "I mustn't get involved in something like that."

"But please," Lydia begged, "just let me tell you about my idea." She got off the bed and came closer to Matty. "This plan will work, I know it.

"You see, on Saturday I'll pretend to have a sudden attack of stomach upset and take to my bed. Then, after a while, I'll start worrying and fussing about being alone here on Sunday morning when everyone goes off to church — well everyone but Tilly and she wouldn't be any help, of course. So, anyway, I would get hysterical and insist that you must come here to look after me."

"Oh, my," Matty tried to interrupt, "that's not —"

Lydia held up her hands for silence and kept right on talking. "When you come here, I'll have clothing all laid out for you to wear and, as soon as everyone leaves the house, we'll quickly get dressed and follow them. Of course, we'll stay out of sight. Once we get to the meeting house, we'll sit on a back bench where my parents won't see us. Then, during the announcement time, before the service begins, you can stand up and tell everyone about the directory." Pleased with herself, the girl settled on the window seat and waited for a reaction.

At a loss for words, Matty simply shook her head. She couldn't believe her ears. What an astonishing idea, she thought, my standing up and addressing an audience — and one where men are present! Women don't do that. I certainly wouldn't dare. To delay responding, she went back to unpacking the trunk.

"Well, what do you think of my plan?" Lydia persisted.

"I don't know what to think," Matty finally said. "I

hope you won't be offended, but there are so many problems with your plan. And, a major one is my getting permission to even come here and miss the morning service at our meeting house."

"Surely, they'd let you come when you explain how ill I am and that you'll only miss the one service. George and Mrs. Dugan always come back here to serve the midday meal and they don't attend the afternoon service."

"I doubt I could get such permission," said Matty. "Besides, wouldn't your mama notice you weren't really sick?"

"She wouldn't come near me. She never wants anything to do with sick people."

"Well, I certainly couldn't stand up in your meeting house and speak to all those people," Matty said. "You should be the one to do that."

"No, you must do it. And, I know you can," Lydia assured her. "You speak very well and you have a way with words. I loved listening to your stories about your family. I feel certain you could make people see how unjust that directory is, get them to do something about it."

For a while, Matty tried politely to point out other stumbling blocks in such a scheme. When she mentioned that she would be forced to sit up in the 'Blacks only' gallery and that she was unwilling to get up and shout down to people below, Lydia quickly countered.

"That won't happen," she said. "You will sit with me and you'll be disguised. No one will see the color of your skin. I've got clothing all planned for that."

"What will you tell your parents when they see you there?" Matty asked.

"I'll just tell them I was feeling better and that you decided to come along."

Oh my, Matty thought, as she placed two more dresses in a drawer. Lydia's ready to lie so easily. And, she's got it all planned out so I'll likely be the one to get the blame.

Becoming annoyed with Matty's reluctance, Lydia took another approach. "You've taught me so much about Negro people, what they suffered and their struggle to get free — and about some of the prejudice going on in this town. I saw your anger that day in the library when you looked at the Boston Directory. I just know you want something to be done to correct it. And I do, too. Don't you see, Matty, this is a good chance for that?"

"I don't know," Matty replied slowly. "It all seems so risky and I don't want to get into trouble. And besides, I really doubt I could do that, stand up and talk to a room full of people."

But, even as those words left her mouth, in the back of Matty's mind, temptation was beginning to nibble. One thought flashed before her. If no one ever speaks up, injustice will only get worse.

Chapter Fifteen
Sunday morning, 12 July

I must be dreaming. I can't believe I'm really doing this, Matty thought, as she carefully pulled on the second white silk stocking. She carefully tied the garter string above the knee.

"Do hurry," Lydia urged quietly. She stood waiting by her open bedroom door. "Everyone's left for church now and we've got to follow as quickly as possible."

Dressing had been a simple thing for Lydia, just a few pieces of light summer clothing, bare legs and soft leather shoes. But Matty's attire was a whole different matter. Putting on those stockings plus a long-sleeved white cotton dress to hide her dark skin had taken some time. And, already she was beginning to perspire. Reluctantly, she covered her neck with a white cotton cloth. Then, picking up white cotton gloves and donning a floppy, broad-brim straw hat with a wide attached green scarf, she faced Lydia.

"This isn't going to work," she fretted. "It's too hot. I'll be roasting."

"Oh, don't worry so much," Lydia responded, adjusting Matty's hat and scarf so they all but covered her face. "Your parasol will keep the sun off and I'll give you my fan to use in church." Looking down at Matty's well-worn shoes, she frowned. "I hope people don't notice those. A pair of mine would have looked so much better if your feet weren't so small. Well, never mind. Let's get going."

"What about Tilly," asked Matty, as they headed for the front stairway.

"Don't bother about her," Lydia responded. "She'll manage until you get back here."

Leaving the house, the girls hurried down to Olive Street. To avoid encountering her parents or their servants, Lydia had planned a roundabout way to South Meeting House near the center of town.

Once across Belknap Street, they then followed Summer Street as it curved back of the State House. As they passed the excavations, stray winds tilted the girls' parasols and sent swirls of red dust over their clothes. Still, they kept hurrying onward, brushing off as best they could. Once they reached Beacon Street, they stopped to look around among a crowd of church goers. Most people were on foot, but a few carriages could be seen.

"There they are," Lydia said quietly pointing to her left along Beacon Street. "Papa's carriage is well ahead of us. We'll just stay back among the crowd until they reach the meeting house and go inside."

Both girls remained silent as they walked along. Matty, keenly aware of her odd head covering, kept shifting her parasol to block people's view.

I can't believe this is real, she thought, that we've managed to get this far. And, I'm still amazed how easy it was getting permission to come up the hill today because of Lydia's 'illness.'

Smiling to herself, she recalled that scene at home last evening. She had come back from work to find their kitchen filled with chattering people, mostly women. They were proudly putting the finishing touches on a great quantity of baking for next Tuesday's anniversary celebration at the

African Meeting House. Nearly every inch of the pine table and even one of the long benches was covered with all sorts of inviting pies and cakes. Ned and several men were seated on the other long bench, admiring the display.

As done on other occasions, the women had come that day to make good use of Bess's two bake ovens – one larger than the other. No other kitchen in the neighborhood had such luxury.

Amid the noise in the room, Matty tried to explain to Bess about Lydia's sudden *'illness'* and that she would be needed at the Bainbridge's on Sunday morning. Her grandmother started to object, but Ned overheard what was going on and decided to step in.

"Bess, there's no great harm in Matty missing one of our church services," he said. "And, she is needed up there."

Bess, perhaps distracted by her work or not wanting to make a scene, simply gave Matty and Ned an annoyed look and waved them away in resignation.

Of course, that night, like so many recently, Matty had lain wide awake, plagued by worry. Silently, she rehearsed her upcoming speech while at the same time telling herself she couldn't possibly do it. Then, feelings of guilt set in. Never before had she lied to her relatives or deceived them in such a way. If her grandmother started asking more questions in the morning, she doubted she could continue the deception. But the next morning, to her amazement, there were no probing questions from anyone before she headed off to work.

Now, waiting on Marlborough Street, a short distance from South Meeting House door, Matty felt panic begin to rise.

Beside her, Lydia seemed full of confidence as they watched the last few people enter the building.

"It's all right now," Lydia said, "we can go in." She took hold of Matty's gloved hand, but Matty pulled back.

"I can't do this," she whispered in anguish. "I'll never get past those two men at the door. They'll see me."

"No they won't," Lydia assured her. "You're all covered up and they can't see your face." She folded down her parasol and inspected the opaque scarf which she had sewn on Matty's hat. It did look a bit strange, the way its ties held the brim close to her ears and let fabric drape well over her face.

"What if people come up close and stare?" Matty hissed.

"I'll just laugh and say my friend has to avoid the sun."

Struggling to calm herself, Matty gripped Lydia's hand and followed her into the meeting house. Moving rapidly past those attendants near the door, Lydia led the way along the back of the crowded sanctuary toward a small isolated, empty wooden bench under a tall window. Settling down, Matty put her folded parasol on the floor. Cautiously, she lifted her head a bit to peer under the scarf at her surroundings. The first floor of the great, high-ceiling, white-painted room contained enclosed pews filled with people in their Sunday finest.

Except for some smaller enclosures at either side, most pews were arranged along the length of the room before the pulpit. There Matty saw an imposing, tower-like structure with a massive paneled wood canopy suspended over it. Below and in front of that pulpit was an elegant table with a deacon's chair at either end. Compared to the atmosphere in her own meeting house, this one seemed far too hushed and formal.

Fighting a sudden urge to run for the door, she gripped the edge of the seat. No, she told herself. I've come this far…and for good reason. I've got to stay calm. In a few minutes, I'll just get up and have my say and then leave as quickly as possible.

Now, throughout the room there came the sound of foot shuffling as the congregation stood up for the entrance of the Reverend Josiah Watson.

As the girls stood, Lydia whispered, "As soon as he gets up front and starts his greeting, I'll get his attention. You follow me."

In preparation for her next move and fearing that her veiling might cause her to stumble, Matty loosened it and pulled it back part way. That action revealed some of her face.

Now, as the minister finished saying "Good morning everyone" and opened his mouth to speak further, Lydia stepped into the center aisle and called out, "If you please, Reverend Watson, my friend has come with an important announcement."

With heads turning at this strange interruption, Matty started forward. Then, from the corner of her eye, she caught sight of one of the front door attendants rapidly moving in her direction. Quickly, she changed course and headed for an aisle on the far side of the room. As she scurried down it, her veiling came undone and her bonnet flew off. It landed in the lap of a startled old gentleman, but Matty kept going. Reaching the front of the room, she came to a halt a short distance from the minister.

A tall man of great dignity, Reverend Watson raised

his hand to quell the commotion sweeping the room. Signaling the pursuing attendant to hold back, he gave Matty a frowning, questioning stare. "I've come to ask for your help," she managed to blurt out. Then she froze at the sight before her. A sea of unsmiling white faces stared back. Anxiously, she looked for support from Lydia, but Mr. Bainbridge already had his daughter by the arm and was swiftly escorting her from the room. In a front row, Mrs B. was slumped against another woman who was frantically waving a fan at her.

"What is this help you seek?" the minister prompted impatiently.

"I…I…," Matty struggled against her fear. "I've come because there's another dreadful injustice being done to us…to African people… and for no other reason than the color of our skin. It's the Boston Town Directory," she hurried on. "Please, everyone, I'm asking you to write letters to the editor, make him change the —"

"This is outrageous," a man interrupted as he stood up in a nearby pew. "Remove her! She has no business here." He started into the center aisle, but a loud voice from high above the room caused him to hesitate.

"You let her speak, preacher. It's important what she's sayin'."

Matty craned her neck to peer up at a small galley located close to the ceiling. There, well above a more spacious second floor gallery, she saw a black man smiling down at her. Looking further, she saw more smiling faces, all of whom had skin coloring resembling her own. Encouraged by their smiles, she straightened her shoulders. Bravely, she looked out over the unfriendly faces in front of her and continued.

"Surely, some of you must see how wrong that directory is. There is no reason to isolate us, to treat us with disdain or to chase us away and to —"

"You must stop now, girl," interrupted the minister. He quickly signaled the attendant forward.

"But, I just...."

She got no further. The attendant grabbed her arm and started hurrying her down the center aisle. But he only did so for a few steps before Matty struggled free, causing them both to come to a stop. Defiantly, she glared at him. Then, raising her head high, she turned and calmly walked down the aisle and out the front door.

Moments later, a short distance from the meeting house, Matty began to shake. She hugged herself as tears of anger and frustration poured forth. Not daring to pause in her agony, she hurried along the now deserted streets, retracing the route back to the Bainbridge house.

Oh, how could I have been so foolish, she silently railed. I accomplished nothing! Maybe...maybe I even made things worse! I should never have gone along with Lydia's ridiculous idea. Now I'll lose my job and never get a reference for another one. And...oh my, what will I ever do if my folks find out about all this!

A short time later, Matty arrived at the house and started to go around back. Then she stopped. "No," she whispered defiantly, "I'm going to use the front door — and the front staircase."

Up in Lydia's bedroom, she quickly changed clothes and went out into the hallway, prepared to hurry down the back stairs. To her surprise, however, there was Tilly easily making her way up those stairs with a generous plate of food.

Tilly quickly hid her own surprise and simply glared angrily. As Matty stepped back to let her pass, she gave the woman a broad grin, enjoying the discovery of a supposedly still infirmed Tilly.

"Get out of my way," Tilly growled, as she moved on toward the third floor stairs. "You tell on me, you'll be sorry."

Matty kept right on grinning as she hurried down the narrow back stairs. Oh, what fun it would be to make trouble for Tilly, she thought. If only I weren't in it myself.

Chapter Sixteen

*H*aving changed from work clothes to proper church attire, Matty sat by the kitchen window, waiting until it was time to go to the afternoon service. She certainly didn't want to join her family during the nooning with all that opportunity for her grandmother's probing questions. Deep in her belly, she felt a sick, sinking sensation. In anguish she whispered, "How will I ever face it...face what's sure to come?"

Much later, in the afternoon, as the family was leaving the meeting house, Bess asked her first question.

"Is that Bainbridge girl very sick?

"Not too much," Matty slowly replied. She carefully avoided looking her grandmother in the eye.

"Does she have any skin rash?" Bess asked.

"No. It's mostly an upset stomach."

"Well," said Bess, "if it's nothing worse, I guess it's all right for you to go back to work there tomorrow."

That last word sent a shock of alarm through Matty. Oh my, she thought. What in the world am I going to do about tomorrow! I certainly don't have a job anymore. And, if I stay home I'll have to invent more lies and... then what?

Her family was about to go for one of their Sunday afternoon walks along the banks of the Charles River or to some other area where they could proceed without incident. It was an occasion dear to Matty's heart, one she looked forward to each week. But not today. Fearing more of Bess's questioning, Matty said, "I'm kinda tired, Gramma. I'd really like to go home and rest if you don't mind."

Giving Matty a puzzled, searching look, Bess finally

nodded her head. "All right, but mind you stay indoors."

Throughout the remainder of that day, as well as far into the night, Matty was plagued by worry. Already ensnared in a web of lies, she knew she must only create more to try and deal with the 'Monday problem'.

It was near dawn when her sleep-deprived mind finally found a solution.

Next morning, at the usual early hour, Matty bid her relatives goodbye and left the house as if going to work. Reaching Belknap Street, she walked part way up and then turned into Mays Court. Grateful at seeing no one around, she quickly entered the African Meeting House and closed the door. All was quiet as she made her way up to the gallery above the deserted sanctuary and then settled down on a front row bench. Extending across the front of it was a waist-high panel which served as a safety railing and now a possible shield for Matty if anyone came into the room below.

She heaved a sigh of relief. So far so good, she thought. I'll just stay here and then at the end of the day, I'll simply go home. That way, no one will know I haven't gone to work. If someone should come in here – and that's most unlikely on a Monday – I'll hide under this bench. Thank goodness the school downstairs is closed until Wednesday.

Pleased with her plan, she reached into her pocket and withdrew a hunk of bread, one she had put there when Bess wasn't looking. Munching small bites, she continued pondering the situation. If I can just get through this day, then maybe everything will be all right. Tonight, I'll simply tell the folks that my job at the Bainbridge's is finished because Tilly's leg is healed. And tomorrow, there'll be the Anniversary Celebration here to keep everyone busy. And after that...well, if I'm lucky, they may not find out what I did.

But what if they do! What if they hear about it today? Oh, it'll be so terrible facing their anger. And, who knows what punishment I'd get.

Various possibilities flashed through her mind. Surely no one would raise a hand to me, she thought. They've never done that...least not since I was little and got a fanny smack sometimes. But I'm sure they won't trust me anymore. I'll be stuck at home again and it'll probably be a long time before they let me get another job.

Looking at the remaining hunk of bread in her hand, she realized she'd better save some for later. As she returned it to her pocket, she touched her handkerchief and felt a lump tied in one corner of it. Withdrawing the cloth, she undid the knot and let some coins slide into her palm — one dollar and sixty-two cents. At least I've got these wages from the last two weeks plus an extra bit for that first Saturday. I wonder if Gramma Bess will make me give all this to her as punishment?

Well, I shouldn't have to, she silently argued. It's mine. I earned it. I can't let Gramma treat me that way. I'm not a child.

Then, unbidden, an idea came to mind. I suppose I could run away... maybe go to Vermont. That's one place where black people are more welcome — at least so I've heard. This money could help me get there. It's not a lot, but it might last until I could find a job.

She gazed around the great, familiar room as if seeking reassurance. Then suddenly she whispered "What a crazy idea! Running away isn't the answer." Besides, she thought, I might be caught by some kidnapper and sold down South. Then I'd really find out what slavery is all about! Oh my, I don't want to leave here...leave my family. There's just got to be some other way out of this trouble. Surely, I can make my family see I didn't mean any harm...that I was only trying to do something good for us.

Feeling miserable and tired, she curled up on the bench and put her head down on her arms. Her eyes felt heavy. It occurred to her that she hadn't really had a proper night's rest in quite a while...certainly not since Friday when Lydia came up with her scheme. I'll just nap right through this day, she thought. That's the way to get past it.

As sleep took hold, she breathed a quiet prayer. "Please, dear God, help me get through this mess and I promise I'll never tell lies again."

Later that evening, the Almighty did seem to be smiling on Matty — or so she believed. All appeared to be going as planned. At the meeting house she had remained undetected and slept most of the day. Awakening a little before sunset, she went home to find a house so filled with people and activity that no one paid more than casual attention to her. Once again, Bess's friends and neighbors were in the kitchen, finishing more food preparations for tomorrow's feast. This time, an inviting display of cooked meats, half a dozen pots of freshly baked beans plus other foods covered most of the long pine table. Their mouth-watering aromas filled the house.

With Bess still quite busy, Matty was put in charge of serving supper. As she brought bowls of mutton stew to her father and uncle who were seated in the only open space at the table, she mentally braced herself, expecting the worst. But they simply greeted her with affection. As for the boarders who had been forced to find seats on the back porch, they accepted their food with only their usual comments.

Now, settling down on a corner of the back porch with her own supper, Matty smiled to herself. I think all my worrying was a waste of time. I haven't noticed even the slightest hint that anyone has heard about my 'adventure' with Lydia.

Chapter Seventeen
Tuesday morning, 14 July

$\mathcal{I}$t was a little past eleven by the time Matty and Ned reached the top of the hill at the corner of Myrtle and Belknap Street. In the distance, from a block or so away, music and a great thumping of drums could be heard. The grand Fourteenth of July Parade was making its way up Russell Street.

Feeling a rush of excitement, Matty grasped her great uncle's out-stretched hand and they hurried to find a place in the waiting crowd of happy on-lookers. Both sides of Myrtle Street were lined with people, mostly women and children come to cheer their men folk.

"Looks like Fortune is smiling on us today," Matty piped up. And, she thought with a touch of guilt, I sure hope old Mister Fortune keeps smiling on me.

Waiting now for a first glimpse of the parade, she hummed to herself while enjoying the cooling shade of an ancient elm tree. Now and then, a breeze lifted her apron and fluttered the edges of her mob cap.

A few hours earlier, such a breeze – ocean born — had swept in from the Charles River and over a field just north of Cambridge Street. There, back of Parkman Market House, nearly three hundred black men in their best attire had assembled for the parade. No doubt they welcomed that cooling breeze on sweating brows.

At ten o'clock, a band struck up a lively tune and the marchers set forth. Parade leaders had planned their route carefully so as not disrupt town traffic any more than necessary. To the rest of Boston, this was just another business day.

Only the black residents understood the need to mark it for celebration.

Marchers proceeded down to busy Cambridge Street and a constable held traffic back while they crossed to Center Street. At that point, the men began winding through North Slope Village streets in a zigzag pattern, making their way up Beacon Hill. Such a peaceful parade should have proceeded unmolested. But it had never been allowed to do so. Since 1808 when it first took place with city permission, the marchers always met with hostile, jeering, white spectators. Gangs of white boys would taunt and threaten them, sometimes throwing rotten eggs or street trash at the marchers.

But none of that ever deterred the black men. They simply tightened their formation and proudly kept on course. They knew that eventually the jackals at their heels would lose interest and drift away.

Now, up on the hill, Matty watched as flag and banner carriers finally appeared and turned the corner onto Myrtle Street. Right behind them came the band, a joyous, informal troop of fiddlers, flutists, horn players and lots of men pounding away on hand-made drums, large and small.

Following the band, came smartly dressed members of community organizations such as the African Masonic Lodge, the African Society and some others. Matty felt a thrill at seeing her handsome father leading the Masons – that is, until she noticed runny egg stains dotting his jacket and those of several other men.

"Uncle Ned, look at that," she shouted, angrily. "Look what those terrible white boys did!"

"Aw, don't fret yourself, girl," he shouted back with a grin. "That's just a badge of courage. That's not stoppin' our celebration."

Last in the line of marchers were groups of male visitors from black communities in Salem, Nantucket, Newburyport and elsewhere. Once the parade turned down Belknap Street, heading for the African Meeting House, Matty, Ned, and the cheering crowd followed.

Later on, in the meeting house, services got underway with a joyful spirit. The Reverend Tobias Jennings' voice resounded through the room as he praised Almighty God for causing Britain and the United States and Denmark to end the Atlantic slave trade. No more would their ships be allowed to transport enslaved human cargo. The congregation sounded its approval with a hearty "Amen."

Following that opening prayer, two violinists played a gentle, quiet melody. Next, an unaccompanied tenor, a black visitor from Nantucket, sang the hymn, *Amazing Grace*. At first, only his voice filled the room with those haunting refrains so meaningful to this anniversary. However, as he started the second verse, many in the congregation began humming along, their sounds vibrating through the entire room. Those who knew the words joined in and the soloist graciously lead them through to the hymn's conclusion. Handkerchiefs then fluttered most everywhere as people dried their tears and smiled.

Up to this point, Matty had been taking great pleasure in her 'belonging place'. But now as a visiting white minister stood up in the pulpit and proceeded to read a Bible passage about honoring the master and being good, humble servants,

Matty's mood gradually changed.

Seated up in the gallery, between Ned and Bess, she began to fret. Despite open windows, the packed area was getting uncomfortably warm.

Leaning close to Ned's ear, she whispered, "Wish this event didn't always cause us to give up our regular pew."

He shrugged, but made no reply.

Moving forward a bit, Matty studied the crowded room below.

As far as she could tell, this was the same anniversary scene as in other years. All the pews, except one in front of the pulpit, were filled with men who had marched in the parade. Gazing at those men, she suddenly thought, it isn't fair that Gramma Bess and her African Ladies Charity aren't allowed down there. They're just as important as the men's groups – maybe more so.

Locating her father among the Masons, she felt a flash of anger at seeing those egg stains still visible on his new brown jacket. How dare those boys do that, she thought. Suddenly, images flooded her mind, not only of her own encounter with such boys two weeks ago, but of other unpleasant people and scenes since then.

Trying not to dwell on that, she gazed further around the room. Her eyes came to rest on that front pew which was filled with white visitors – prosperous-looking men and women. Before she could stop herself, she thought, I don't know why they always insist on being separated from the rest of us. And, how come we always have a visiting white minister on this anniversary? Our Reverend Jennings should be conducting the entire service. He knows better than they do what this celebration means to us.

Realizing the direction of her thoughts, Matty's conscience took hold. I shouldn't be thinking this way. If I'm not careful, I'll become as bad as Mrs. Dugan and Tilly.

However, once the visiting minister was well into his sermon, Matty found she couldn't avoid thinking about matters of white versus black.

As usual, when it came to sermons, she had been listening with only half an ear and letting her thoughts drift. At one point, her stomach growled loudly, reminding her of that wonderful anniversary feast waiting in the school room below. Gradually, though, some of the minister's words caught her attention and she found herself listening more closely.

It pleased her to hear him praise local African charity groups when discussing the story of the Good Samaritan. And her interest held as he began speaking of the evils of slavery and the wicked men involved. When he mentioned the disgrace of slavery still going on in the South, Matty eagerly waited for his next sentence. But the one she hoped for did not come. He made no resounding, rallying call to confront government – federal or states — to put an end to such terrible suffering.

Instead, the minister simply moved on. He told his black listeners how grateful they should be to live in this land of peace and plenty with all the opportunities it offers. Sometimes referring to them as *humble* Africans, the minister said they must always guard against idleness and sin. They must make every effort to prove to the public that they were *worthy* to be free.

Further, he told them, they would likely always be in

the lowest rank of public society, but they shouldn't be unhappy about that. And, he hastened to caution them, they must guard against becoming envious or discontent because white people are richer and have more power than they do.

Matty couldn't believe her ears. She wanted to throw up her hands in disgust — especially at that last statement. But of course, with Gramma Bess right beside her, she controlled herself. Glancing up at Ned, she took satisfaction in seeing his clenched jaw and an angry face which mirrored her own. If Bess was angry, her face betrayed no emotion at all.

What bothered Matty even more, was that all during the minister's disdainful and racist statements, no one seemed to be reacting. If there were any murmurs of disapproval among the congregation, she hadn't heard them. From that moment on, all she could think was, I can't wait to get out of this place!

It was just after the service ended that 'old Mister Fortune' decided to frown on Matty. Trouble finally caught up with her – that trouble she'd been dreading. And, there was no escaping the awful moment when it did.

Leaving the gallery, ahead of her relatives, she moved through the crowd and down the west staircase as quickly as she could. She hoped to get an early place in the food line, but got no further than the bottom step where the line ended. Ned was a few steps behind her. Standing there waiting, Matty looked back up to the top of the stairs. There was trouble staring down at her from her grandmother's angry eyes.

Bess was being delayed by two women, the neighborhood's worst gossips. From the pleased look on their faces, it was clear they were taking delight in conveying bad news.

Bess's expression could only be described as thunderous. She leaned over the railing and caught Ned's attention, signaling him to come back up to her.

Oh my, I'm going to get it now, Matty thought, wishing for some way to escape. But before that could happen, Ned returned.

"I don't know what you did, but you must be in a heap of trouble," he said, coming to stand beside her. "I've never seen your gramma so furious. She said you and I are to get our food as quick as possible and then I'm to take you right home. And, you're not to go anywhere until she and your papa get there."

Much later, curled up in a corner of her bed against the wall, Matty waited for Bess's return. Behind the closed door and muffled by a pillow, she had cried until her head was stuffy and aching. Over and over, she blamed first herself and then Lydia. Why was I so foolish, she agonized. Why didn't I just insist on writing a letter! I should never have gone along with Lydia's ridiculous scheme…never let her talk me into such wicked deceitfulness, either. Oh, I dearly wish I'd never met that girl!

Now, with the sun getting low in the sky, she wondered what was delaying her folks. Waiting was a punishment in itself. She longed to get it all over with.

"Matty," Ned called out as he knocked at her door, "you come along now. The folks are home."

Doing as she was told, Matty followed her uncle into the kitchen to find her father and grandmother seated on the far side of the table. Their angry expressions made her feel ill. She stayed by the doorway, uncertain what to do. Ned went over to the fireplace mantel and began filling his pipe. The only other person in the silent room was old Hugger. He was fast asleep in a chair by the window. After a day of such feasting, it appeared that no one was bothering about supper.

Finally, Peter broke the stillness, his voice quiet, but forceful. "Matty, I'm astonished at you! What on earth made you do such a thing?" Not waiting for an answer, he continued, "You've brought disgrace on us. Made us look foolish among our friends and neighbors...and white society beyond this hill."

Feeling dreadful, Matty looked away from his face and then into that of her grandmother.

"I don't know how you can look me in the eye, after doing such an outrageous thing," Bess sputtered angrily. "And, telling us all those lies! I should never have let you go up there to work. I just knew there'd be trouble."

Matty remained silent.

"Well?" demanded Bess, "what do you have to say for yourself,"

Struggling not to cry, Matty said in a halting voice, "I...I didn't mean to do any harm. It's just that...I get so discouraged with all the prejudice against us and nothing's being done to change that. And, after I told you what I saw in that Boston Directory, you didn't seem bothered about that...how wrong it is."

"Oh, that's foolishness," said Bess. "Besides, one person isn't going to change that directory — certainly not a young girl like you. Land sakes! Wherever did you get such a notion?"

"She gets it from her papa," said Ned as he came over and settled down on the bench near where Matty was standing.

"Uncle, what are you talking about," Peter asked with a frown.

"She's just like you were at this age," responded Ned, "wantin' to do battle with every injustice. And you sure took greater risks than Matty has. Many a time we thought the master would sell you away 'cause of your arguing with him. Of course I suppose, in the end, if it wasn't for you keeping at him, we might not have gotten our freedom when we did."

Peter's annoyed expression faded a bit. "I guess you're right, Uncle. But that was different. I was a boy. I don't think old Mr. Warren would have paid any attention if I'd been a girl."

"Oh, Papa!"

"Now, Matty, I didn't mean to hurt your feelings," Peter said. "But you have to face reality. There are some things in this world that are men's concerns and others that are women's."

"Well, you and Ned certainly aren't helping her with that," said Bess. "...all those books you keep letting her read, filling her head with that philosophy and history stuff!"

"Aw, that's not gonna harm her," Ned responded loudly. "She'll just be a better parent for her children some day. Make certain they get a proper education."

Matty hated hearing argument between her great uncle and grandmother, something they seemed to do more often these days. She sifted about in her mind for a way to distract them, get them onto another subject. And, maybe even lead everyone away from her misdeeds.

"Papa," she ventured shyly, "... about that minister's sermon today...I don't understand why people weren't angry with him. It looked to me like they didn't mind what he said about us."

"Of course they did," Peter replied. "I certainly did. But, Matty, I guess you haven't been paying attention to other anniversary sermons. That white minister wasn't saying anything different than what we've heard before from such visitors. You shouldn't let any of that bother you."

"But, in our own meeting house," Matty responded. "Shouldn't someone at least have indicated their disapproval?"

"What good would that do," Peter said crossly. "We would just offend the white visitors and cause trouble for ourselves. Don't you see yet, Matty? Don't you see why we're so upset by what you did? Behavior like yours isn't going to help us. It could even set us back, lose what respect we've gained from white people. And besides, many of us are dependent on them for our living."

Matty's tears finally gushed forth and she slumped down on the bench beside Ned. He leaned over and gently patted her shoulder. For a few moments, Matty's sobbing was the only sound in the room. Then, collecting herself, she raised her head and looked over at her father.

"I guess Uncle Ned is right. It really is hopeless for us in this country. Our freedom doesn't mean anything. We'll never have a better life."

"Now, now, Matty," said her father, "you mustn't give up hope. We are making progress. You just don't realize how much. If you hadn't been so young when we got our freedom, you'd see how far we've come. Most of us started out with nothing…little more than the shirt on our backs. But, we've built a whole community here with the meeting house and its school…and charity groups to help our people. But progress takes time, Matty, and patience on everyone's part."

"Matty," Bess spoke up, her voice stern, "just where did you go yesterday? I can't believe you went to work. You certainly wouldn't have been welcome at the Bainbridges after what you did."

Feeling trapped, Matty hesitated before replying. "No, Gramma, I didn't go there. I...um...I spent the day sitting in our meeting house."

"What? You did what?" Bess cried out. "I'm astonished at you! Deceiving us like that. And," she sputtered, "that on top of all the lies you've told us! How can we ever trust you again!"

"Huh...huh?" Hugger suddenly started up from his sleep. Bess's loud outcry must have awakened him. Yawning and stretching, he stood up on wobbly legs and then shuffled across the room to Peter and Bess. Hugging each of them, he mumbled his one and only phrase, "Bless ya. Bless ya." Then he went around the table to do the same for Ned. When he reached Matty, he stopped to look her in the eye. Then grinning, he gave her a tight hug. "Bless ya. Bless ya...good Matty girl."

Everyone simply stared in astonishment, watching as that elderly man left the kitchen and slowly climbed the steep steps to the loft.

"He spoke my name," Matty whispered in wonder.

Ned smiled broadly and shook his head. "I've always suspected that old man could say more if he wanted to. Guess you must be really special, Matty."

A short time later, when everyone had gone off to bed, Hugger's special blessing continued to comfort Matty. Of course, as Bess had sternly informed her, her troubles were not over. There would be more 'discussion' in the morning. Now, staring out the window into a dark moonless night, Matty tried to settle into sleep. She listened, hoping the only sound from the other bed would soon be her grandmother's soft snoring.

But Bess broke the silence in a stern, but quiet voice. "I'm still waiting."

"For what, Gramma?"

"You still haven't apologized to me for all the lies you've told."

"Oh, Gramma. I do feel awful about that. I really am sorry."

"And…," Bess prompted.

"And I promise I'll never do that again." Turning on her side to face away, Matty thought…but, I don't want to apologize for going to South Meeting House. In spite of what Papa said, I can't help thinking I might possibly have done some good…got at least a few people to realize the wrong being done to us.

Chapter Eighteen
Thursday, 23 July

Now and then, a fickle sort of breeze ruffled glistening waters around Hancock's Wharf. It hummed among the rigging of several ships beside it while playfully scattering bits of litter and dust over the pier's broad timbers.

Matty shaded her eyes against the afternoon sun, searching for Lydia among a crowd of people and piles of cargo beside one of the ships.

Standing at a short distance from the crowd with her uncle Ned beside her, Matty self-consciously smoothed wrinkles from her new blue gingham dress – the one she had hastily finished sewing last night. She felt only excitement at the prospect of seeing her hill-top acquaintance again. Forgotten was the fact that, until several days ago, she never would have imagined being allowed to do so – or even have wanted to.

According to a brief note from Lydia which arrived four days ago, she told Matty that because of their misadventure, she was being 'banished' to Portsmouth, New Hampshire, to stay with her mother's sister. However, she begged Matty to come and meet her at this wharf so they could say goodbye before the ship sailed. After that, she simply signed the note, 'Your most devoted friend, Lydia Bainbridge.'

At first, Matty felt only anger as she read the note…anger at this so-called 'friend' and at being reminded of their wrongdoing. Bess took one look and told her to throw it in the fire. But Matty resisted that and put the note in her pocket, instead. She had never received mail before and it seemed odd to just throw it away.

Later, sitting on the back porch while watching Ned tend their vegetable patch, she re-read Lydia's words several times. Slowly, her anger diminished. Lifting her head to gaze up the hill, she found herself re-calling Lydia's smiling face. Scenes of their more pleasant times together came drifting through her mind.

I guess it is wrong to be so cross with Lydia, she thought. I don't believe she really meant to cause me trouble. She did seem sincere in wanting to know about black people, our problems and all. And, she did save me from that awful gang of boys. It's kind of sad to think I'll never see her again.

Watching Ned at his weeding, Matty suddenly had idea. Maybe if I talk to him, he would see that there couldn't be any harm in my meeting Lydia just one last time. Then he might talk to Gramma Bess and Papa and convince them of that.

As might be expected, once soft-hearted Ned did sympathize and agreed to help, it did take quite a bit of persuasion to get Peter's consent — even more of that, to overcome Bess's objections.

But now, here on the wharf, looking among the crowd of passengers, Matty felt a rush of gratitude toward her uncle.

"There's Lydia," she suddenly said, tugging at Ned's sleeve. "And…." Matty's smile vanished. "Mr. Bainbridge is with her." Guess there won't be much chance for us to talk, she thought. And maybe, I'm simply going to get a scolding from him.

Just then, Lydia looked up and waved to Matty. Turning and saying something to her father, she left him and hurried forward.

"Oh, Matty, I'm so happy you came. I was afraid I'd never see you again." Lydia looked inquiringly at Ned.

"Lydia, may I present my great uncle, Ned Smith," Matty said.

"How do you do," Lydia responded, giving Ned a warm smile.

Matty then touched Ned's hand. "Uncle," she said, "would it be all right if Lydia and I spoke together for a little while?"

"Oh sure," he responded. "I expect you girls must have lots to talk about. I'll just wait over there." He indicated a wooden piling some distance away and began walking toward it.

For a moment or so, neither girl spoke. Then Lydia said, "Matty, I want you to know how badly I feel about what happened. Did your folks find out? Are they terribly angry with you?"

"Yes, they did…and they are." Matty looked grim. "Guess it'll be a long time before Gramma Bess stops lecturing me about that. I kind of wish I were sailing away from all of it like you are. Will you be gone long?"

"I don't think so," said Lydia, holding her bonnet against the breeze. "Maybe for a few months." Then she grinned. "Of course Mama might want that to be longer. She's so furious. She says our reputation is completely ruined and we should move to another town. But Papa won't let that happen. He says, once I'm out of sight for a while, the scandal will be forgotten.

"It's really all my fault," said Matty. "If only I had never gone up Beacon Hill that day, you and I would never have met and then done such a foolish thing."

"Never have met? Oh, no, Matty," said Lydia. "I'm ever

so glad we did meet. You taught me so much…things I will always remember. From now on when I see Negro people, I will see them and think about them in such a different way. And, Matty, you can't take all the blame for what we did. I was the one who came up with that scheme. We should have just written a letter the way you wanted to."

"Well, none of that matters now," Matty said with a sigh. She looked out across the wharf, thinking of that Sunday two weeks ago.

"Lydia," she ventured shyly, "do you think there was anyone at all in your meeting house who cared about what I was trying to do… other than those people way up in the top gallery?"

"Perhaps. But I haven't heard anything," the girl replied. "And, of course I don't dare ask."

"Do you believe in fate, Lydia?"

"Can't say that I do."

"Sometimes," Matty said, "I have this feeling that you and I were meant to meet. Do what we did. And just maybe, when we're older and wiser, each of us will find some other opportunity to help white people see the error of their ways."

"Yes, said Lydia brightly, "…and we might even do that together."

"Oh, I doubt that," replied Matty. "Most likely, we won't ever meet again." She glanced over Lydia's shoulder, noticing that most passengers were now aboard the ship and men were beginning to raise one of the sails.

There was an awkward pause in their conversation. Then Lydia spoke up. "At least we could write letters to one another while I'm away"

"I...I don't think that's a good idea," said Matty. "That would probably cause more trouble at home for me." Her grandmother's stern words that morning came to mind. *You listen here, Matty. After today, I don't want you having anything to do with that girl — ever again!*

Lydia reached out and took hold of Matty's hand. "I enjoyed the time we had together and I won't ever forget you. Perhaps one day, when we can do as we wish, we will get together again...that is if your family doesn't go off to Africa or somewhere."

"I don't know about leaving," Matty replied. "From everything Papa says, I believe he wants us to stay here... that despite what's going on, we do have a right to be here, same as everyone else." Hesitating a moment, she added, "but, if rumors are true, the government might find a way to force free black people to leave someday."

"I dearly hope there's no truth to that," said Lydia. "Surely, our government would never do such an unjust and cruel thing."

Annoyed at Lydia's unthinking remark, Matty withdrew her hand from the girl's grasp. She prepared to argue, remind Lydia of the government's real behavior toward black people. But Mr. Bainbridge prevented that. Down near the ship, she saw him turn and beckon toward them.

In a dull voice she said, "You need to go now, Lydia. Your father wants you."

Lydia seemed not to notice the change in Matty's attitude. Instead, she smiled and said hastily, "Goodbye now, Matty. Keep well...and I intend to keep hoping we meet again."

For her part, Matty merely responded, "Goodbye,

Lydia. I hope you have a safe voyage."

As the girl hurried away, Ned came over to stand beside Matty. He put a comforting arm around her shoulders. Silently, they watched as Lydia hugged her father, gave a last wave in Matty's direction and then scampered up the gangplank.

"I don't think we ought to linger here," said Ned. "We'd be wise to leave and get on home before dark."

During the long walk back through town, there was little conversation between them. Ned was intent on safely weaving their way through the narrow, busy streets while avoiding dangerous carriage wheels and flying horses' hooves. It was a danger that could be made worse if they should encounter some hostile white pedestrian demanding right of way on the sidewalk. This afternoon, however, they were able to keep to their path without incident.

Hurrying along, Matty's mind kept going back to that scene on the wharf and watching Lydia ascend the gangplank. I don't think that girl looked unhappy at all at her banishment, she thought. She boarded that ship so confidently, so sure of herself...so certain of her place in the world. How I wish I could be like that. Maybe we'll never be rich the way her family is, but it would be truly wonderful to at least have public respect wherever we go.

She sighed aloud and Ned heard it. He turned and gave her a questioning look, but said nothing. Oh, I know, she silently told herself, it is wicked to be discontented all the time. But how can I help that. There's such an ocean of difference between Lydia and me — just because of the color of our skin!

Nearing home, they crossed Belknap Street and Ned

slowed down to a more relaxed pace. "I sure hope Bess has supper ready," he said. "I'm so hungry I could eat six chickens, feathers and all."

Matty laughed and tugged at his hand. She loved the way he always seemed to come up with a funny remark just when she needed one. As they walked past the alleyway leading to the African Meeting House, Matty glanced up and saw its third story windows aglow with afternoon sun. She felt her spirits lift even more. My *belonging place*, she thought fondly. Guess it is childish to keep thinking of that building in such a way. But, after all, it's been the center of my life since we came here – church, community gatherings and nearly five years of school.

Suddenly she thought, I went to the wrong place to try and change things. I should have gone to our meeting house. Surely, if enough people there got upset they might be able to do something about that Boston Directory. I don't think we should just give up.

Maybe, in a few weeks, when Papa isn't still so cross with me, I could talk to him about that again. See if there isn't something that can be done.

ACKNOWLEDGEMENTS

I am most grateful to the following people for their help-fulness in the research and writing of this book. Liz Nelson, historian, author and editor, kept asking all the right questions. I cannot thank her enough for her insight and willing, patient help over the last four years. Valerie Cunningham and Mark Sammons, co-authors of *BLACK PORTSMOUTH: Three Centuries of African American Heritage*, once again gave me the benefit of their extensive knowledge. Also, I am indebted to Joanne Pope Melish, PhD, author of *DISOWNING SLAVERY: Gradual Emancipation and "Race" in New England, 1780-1860*, for her encouraging and helpful comments on the manuscript. A special thank you is due to the American Antiquarian Society Library and the Reference Department of the Portsmouth Public Library, especially Kate Giordano. Amazing what can be accomplished through inter-library loan systems.

My family, Brad, Larry and especially Valerie, kept me steady against those blustery winds of writer's doubt and worry. Other people who kindly took the time to read and comment on various drafts of this book include: Trudy Anderson, Merrie Craig, Rose Eppard, L'Merchie Frazier, Education Director, Museum of African American History, Boston, The Reverend Jeffrey M. Gallagher, The Right Reverend Barbara C. Harris, Bishop Suffragan of Massachusetts (retired), Jackie Hinton, Vernis Jackson, President of Portsmouth's Seacoast African American Cultural Center, Corinne Mann, Elizabeth Morgan, Charlene Rathbun, Deborah A. Richards, Debby Ronnquist, Freddye Ross, Jill Seabrook, Olivia Schneider, Grant Smith, Jane Uscilka, Beverly Morgan Welch, Executive Director, Museum of African American History in Boston, and Natali Wall.

Afterthoughts

This fictional story is merely a hint, a glimpse of that disheartening and growing racism which confronted black people after they gained their freedom in New England. BEYOND FREEDOM was written as a tribute to a people who refused to be daunted; who gathered their courage to begin the struggle for a rightful place in America and, eventually, for abolition of slavery.

By 1832, with the founding of the New England Anti-Slavery Society in the African Meeting House, black women as well as black men became involved in the Abolitionist Movement. Though history records more about men's activities, women were a mainstay for the cause through fund-raising suppers, craft fairs and other public events. Some joined the Boston Female Anti-Slavery Society, helped organize other abolitionist groups and joined in public protests. And, black women bravely defied the law by giving aid and shelter to people fleeing from Southern slavery. Eventually, some nineteenth century black women became public speakers and writers not only for abolition but for civil rights and women's rights.

Facts of the Matter

This story may have left you with questions as to what was truth and what was fiction. Below, by page number from the book, are brief answers. Many of these, however, are like icebergs. Below the surface are larger and important stories regarding early African American history in New England. I hope that you will be encouraged to discover them. A selected bibliography follows this section.

Though the story, characters, and house locations are fictional, its setting is based on a real neighborhood – sometimes referred to as the North Slope Village — that once existed on Beacon Hill in Boston. In 1812 it included an area from about Myrtle Street to Cambridge Street and from Belknap (now Joy Street) almost to the Charles River. The 1806 African Meeting House, home of the First Baptist Church, was the center of black religious, social and educational life at the time of this story. Later, it became a major center for the anti-slavery movement in New England. This historic building is now in the keeping of the Museum of African American History in Boston.

As to various racial, economic and social problems touched upon in this story, I have relied on published sources and some archival material. Though much is known about the later years of the Beacon Hill black community – 1830s onward – information is scarce regarding it formative years. Even earliest records of the First Baptist Church are lost.

In order to convey a reasonably realistic description of living conditions in the North Slope Village c.1812, I consulted numerous sources. Among them, John Blake's PUBLIC HEALTH in the TOWN OF BOSTON, 1630-1822 (Harvard University Press, 1959), Josiah Quincy's MUNICIPAL HISTORY OF THE TOWN AND CITY OF BOSTON (Boston, 1852) and Town Selectmen's Minutes give evidence of serious and long-standing sanitation problems in much of the town – especially in poorer, overcrowded neighborhoods. The town's methods of dealing with those problems were still primitive and at times inconsistent and ineffective. Residents with money, however, could alleviate some of those problems. In modern times we have sewers for all wastes, but at that time, Boston dealt only with rainwater run-off through buried pipes or above-ground street drains.

For North Slope Village and West Boston c.1812, everything points to an area under environmental stress. Not only were residents living with primitive sanitation and long-term industrial pollution, the gradual filling of the old mill pond was creating more unpleasant, unhealthful problems for them.

As for the manner of speaking for my characters, I let it reflect their level of education. Blacks who had opportunity to learn proper English spoke it. Others, less educated, spoke broken or incorrect English – just as their white counterparts would have. Though African dialects influenced many blacks' speech, I lacked the knowledge to portray that in an accurate way.

A further note: young students may wonder why I used so many designations for people – Africans, Negroes, blacks, people of color. All of those terms were in use at that time. It's apparent from the names of organizations that many blacks thought of themselves primarily as Africans.

Notations

Page 7 – Belknap Street, now Joy Street, was once far more steep than it is today. Doubtless its sharp incline c.1812 would have been an unpleasant challenge.

Page 7 – After 1783, as Massachusetts enslaved blacks were getting their freedom, many began settling in one of the few places available to them – the less desirable, steep, sandy north slope of Beacon Hill. By 1798, people began referring to the settlement as a Negro village. Some blacks were able to buy a bit of land and build a small house. Later, many others found shelter in newly built rental houses or in crowded tenements. As far as is known, only a small portion of such property was owned by blacks.

Please note: slavery in Massachusetts finally came to an end primarily through the efforts of several enslaved women and men who, over the years, successfully sued their masters in court for their freedom. In 1781 the case brought by Quok Walker against his master had to make its way through various courts until, in 1783, a Massachusetts Supreme Court justice ruled that slavery was incompatible with the state's constitution. However, no clear law banning slavery followed that court decision so it took several more years before Massachusetts whites, in law and custom, fully and completely acknowledged blacks' freedom.

Page 10 — As later revealed in this story, Bess is mistaken about the nature and continuing enforcement of a 1757 law regarding access to Boston Common by people of color. That law banned "Indian, Negro and Mulatto slaves and servants" from the Common and public streets during the Sabbath and at certain other times. With the ending of slavery in the state, such a law would likely have gone out of enforcement. But its' long-time existence would have shaped some whites' attitude and behavior toward blacks. Actual repeal of the law did not occur until well into the 19th century.

Page 14 — Taking in boarders for extra income was common in this neighborhood. As to rope making, it required a coating of strong-smelling, oily tar for strength and water-proofing. Rope factories, long wooden sheds called ropewalks, had been common in the northern Beacon Hill area.

Page 14 — In 1810, a Federal law excluded blacks from "conveying the mails." This came about over white fear that free blacks might become too knowledgeable of public affairs and rights and possibly form political alliances with other blacks.

Page 16 — The name of Bess's charitable group is fictional, but there seems little doubt that black women in those earliest years would have been involved in community self-help efforts. They also likely played at least a back-up role in the charitable work of men-only organizations such as the African Masonic Lodge and the African Society (founded 1796). A bit later in the 19th century, black women formed their own charitable and cultural organizations.

Page 16 – At that time no Boston orphanage would accept black children.

Page 17 – The removal or "warning out" of vagrants and impoverished non-residents from town was a practice of long standing in New England. By the turn of the nineteenth century, Boston apparently was concerned about the increase of unemployed free blacks coming into town from other parts of the state, the West Indies and the South. Anxious to avoid having to provide charitable aid to such newcomers, town authorities sought ways to remove them. Police in each ward were instructed to make weekly reports of "vagrants, disorderly persons and strangers of suspicious character." A further notation requested reports on "all persons not proper inhabitants of the town and who are indigent and are not householders in town." In 1800 a list of several hundred people of color was published in newspapers, warning them to leave town or face severe punishment. Among them were quite a number of longtime residents of Boston.

Page 17 – Though major streets usually had buried drains, side streets and alleyways often had a shallow rainwater drain down the middle. Many of these were partially covered by removable stone slabs.

Page 21 — Peter's comment about kidnapping is based on fact. That was a real danger for free blacks in the north. His remarks regarding other dangers on some Boston streets are also based on fact.

Page 22 – Regarding the law and Boston Common, see notation for Page 13.

Pages 23 – The discussion regarding the state of slavery at that time is based on fact.

Page 24 — It is true that part of the funds for building the African Meeting House came from some white residents who probably lived elsewhere in Boston. As to the argument between Bess and Ned there was, at that time, a sincere belief among some (perhaps many) black people that they could eventually over-come white prejudice simply by changes in speech, personal appearance and social behavior.

Reference is made to Captain Paul Cuffee, a wealthy black merchant and ship owner of Massachusetts. In the spring of 1812, he sent a letter to black friends in Boston regarding preparation for an expedition for re-settlement in Sierra Leone, Africa. However, his plans were delayed until the War of 1812 ended.

Page 30 — Doubtless, the reduction of the huge Monument Hill caused problems for Beacon Hill residents – especially down in Matty's neighborhood. It would be many years before the mill pond was filled and locals stopped complaining about swampy odors and sewer problems. Today, Massachusetts General Hospital occupies most of the pond site.

Page 35 — Ned's comment about manure is based on fact. Removal of it was a continual, major problem which residents — until the 1820s — either solved privately or endured the town's somewhat inept methods. For most of the year, manure seems to have been left on the streets to be carried away by rain or melting snow. In spring, farmers were encouraged to come whenever they wished to cart away what manure they needed. By 1823 when a new city government was formed, the mayor reported that, in a single month, twenty-eight hundred tons of manure had been removed from Boston's streets.

Page 50 — Lydia's mention of "wicked people" refers to a disreputable area on the far western slope of Beacon Hill close to the Charles River. It had long been a location of establishments for gambling, drinking and other vice. However, Matty's home was nearly five blocks away from that area.

Page 53 — The family stories which Matty begins telling to Lydia are, though fiction, based on some typical experiences of enslaved blacks in New England. A fuller version of those fictional stories can be found in my first book, *Child Out of Place: A Story of New England.*

Page 59 — Matty's descriptions reveal style change in furnishings and architecture then taking place under the direction of architect Charles Bulfinch. The stewing stove was part of a new fireplace cooking arrangement called a Rumford Kitchen. Its use, however, was short lived. In 1820, free-standing cast iron stoves began replacing it. One of the few surviving Rumford Kitchens can be seen today in Historic New England's Rundlet-

May House in Portsmouth, New Hampshire.

Page 67 — This scene in the meeting house is entirely imaginary. Little seems to be known about the appearance of the original interior. Diarist William Bentley mentioned in 1806 that it was being built in the "usual way" with a gallery, pews and benches and that it did have a first floor or basement beneath the sanctuary for various uses.

It is reasonable to assume there would have been religious and cultural differences among this early congregation. The first minister, the Reverend Thomas Paul, grew up and was ordained in New Hampshire. Doubtless, he followed old New England religious practices. And, many of his congregation had been born into or indoctrinated by those same religious traditions. However, with an influx of blacks from the West Indies and the South, there would have been variations in worshipers' needs and attitudes. Many in that newer group had not been forced to abandon African religious traditions.

Celebrating the July 14th anniversary of the end of the slave trade was most important to blacks in Boston and elsewhere in the North. And, despite the white public's disdain, observance of that occasion continued for some years.

In this chapter, the characters' comments and attitudes reflect what was apparently worrying free black people at that time. Doubtless, arguments arose among them over the 'stay or go' idea. For a number of years, some free blacks had been seeking ways and funds to re-settle in Africa, to leave a country so scornful and often hostile to them. But others would have staunchly argued for staying, for claiming their rightful citizenship in the country in which they had been born.

As to rumors in 1812 that some government authority was going to force free blacks to leave the country, I believe those were likely. For quite some time, various prominent white men and government leaders had been discussing what they perceived as the 'free black problem' – how it might be controlled or eliminated. That 1810 law prohibiting black postal workers seems clear evidence of the direction of their thinking. By 1816, deliberations led to formation of the American Colonization Society whose sole aim was to raise money to remove as many free blacks as possible from the nation. Chapters of that Society soon sprang up in towns throughout New England.

Page 72 – 'Nooning', the gathering together between Sunday services, was an old New England tradition more commonly done in rural areas where people lived at some distance from the meeting house.

Page 74 – There is truth in Ned's opinion. A sudden ending of slavery would probably have had a disastrous effect on U.S. economy at that time – north as well as south. Sad to say, almost from the beginning, much of our nation's economy was – directly or indirectly — powered by slavery. New England's lucrative maritime trade had long been based on the existence of slave labor in the West Indies and the South. Plantation owners concentrated on producing sugarcane, molasses, rice, tobacco and cotton. New Englanders kept them going by supplying trade goods and more enslaved Africans. Lumber, shoes, iron tools, clothing, dried fish, etc. were shipped south to exchange for local crops, especially molasses for rum production – a major industry in some northern cities such as

Boston. By the beginning of the 19th century, with a huge increase in the number of slaves imported to the south, a greatly increased cotton production began fueling a growing textile industry in the north – primarily New England.

A pamphlet calling for an end to slavery was published by the African Society in Boston in 1808. References to Prince Hall founding the African Masonic Lodge and his initiating a petition to the Massachusetts government for money to go to Africa are factual.

Page 89 – In 1779 some Portsmouth enslaved men did petition the New Hampshire Assembly for their freedom but were unsuccessful.

Page 95 – By 1800, Boston was beginning to go all out for July 4th celebrations, including fireworks displays. And, the town did require an hour of celebratory steeple bell ringing beginning at 6 a.m.

Page 110 – Massachusetts was legally involved in slavery and slave trading from 1641 onward.

Page 112 – Information regarding the Boston Town Directory is correct, except for the date used in my story. The Directory actually began its separate listing of 'Africans' in 1813. Such segregated listing continued for decades.

Page 127 – This scene in South Meeting House is pure invention and has no basis in fact. At that time it would have been unheard of for a woman or a girl to address a public audience, especially where men were present. In 1831 a woman, Maria W. Stewart, a Boston African American abolitionist and writer, broke that social taboo by formally addressing a public audience of men and women. She is credited with being the first woman in America – black or white – to do so.

Page 137 – This chapter is based on what is known about the July 14th celebrations in Boston's black community. Though I found no detailed, first-hand account, the event usually involved a large parade of black men and then a solemn church service at the African Meeting House. There were some white visitors, including a white minister invited to give a special sermon. Following the service there was much feasting, musical entertainment and dancing. And, yes, that occasion was generally treated by Boston's white public with disdain, derision and occasional open hostility.

As to the white minister's condescending and racist comments in this chapter, they were drawn in part from two printed sermons which were given in the African meeting house in 1808 and 1811.

Selected Bibliography

Farrow, Anne; Joel Lang; Jenifer Frank. **COMPLICITY: How the North Promoted, Prolonged and Profited From Slavery** (New York: Ballentine Books, 2005)

Greene, Lorenzo, **THE NEGRO IN COLONIAL NEW ENGLAND** (New York: Columbia University Press, 1942)

Horton, James Oliver, and Lois E. Horton, **IN HOPE OF LIBERTY: Culture, Community and Protest Among Free Blacks, 1700-1860** (Oxford and New York: Oxford University Press, 1997)

Litwack, Leon F., **NORTH OF SLAVERY: The Negro in the Free States: 1790-1860** (Chicago: University Press of Chicago)

Melish, Joanne Pope, **DISOWNING SLAVERY: Gradual Emancipation and "Race" In New England 1780-1860** (Ithaca and London: Cornell University Press, 1998)

Moore, George H., **NOTES ON THE HISTORY OF SLAVERY IN MASSACHUSETTS** (New York: D. Appleton & Company, 1866)

Pierson, William D., **BLACK YANKEES: Development of an Afro-American Subculture in Eighteenth-Century New England** (Amherst: University of Massachusetts Press, 1988)

Sammons, Mark J., and Valerie Cunningham, **BLACK PORTSMOUTH: Three Centuries of African American Heritage** (Durham: University of New Hampshire Press with University Press of New England, 2004)

Staudenraus, Paul J., **THE AFRICAN COLONIZATIONIST MOVEMENT 1816-1865** (New York: Columbia University Press, 1961)

Sources for Boston and the North Slope Village:

Benton, Josiah, **WARNING OUT IN NEW ENGLAND 1656-1817** (Boston: W.B. Clark Company, 1911)

Blake, John B., **PUBLIC HEALTH IN THE TOWN OF BOSTON 1630-1822** (Cambridge: Harvard University Press, 1956)

Boston Records Commissioners' Reports, **BOSTON SELECTMEN'S RECORDS 1776-1810** (Boston: Rockwell & Churchill, 1890)
_____, **BOSTON TOWN RECORDS 1776-1810**
_____, **BOSTON TOWN RECORDS 1784-1796**

BOSTON TOWN DIRECTORY 1813 (Boston: Edward Cotton, Publisher, 1813)

Bower, Beth Anne, "**Material Culture in Boston: The Black Experience.**" In ARCHAEOLOGICAL PERSPECITVES ON ETHNICITY IN AMERICA, R. L. Schuyler, editor, pp. 55-63 (Farmington, NY: Baywood Publishing Company)

Bower, Beth Anne, and Byron Rushing, "**The African Meeting House: The Center for the 19th Century Afro-American Community in Boston.**" In ARCHAEOLOGICAL PERSPECTIVES ON ETHNICITY IN AMERICA, R.L. Schuyler, editor, pp. 69-75 (Farmington, NY: Baywood Publishing Company)

Chamberland, Allen, **BEACON HILL: Its Ancient Pasture and Early Mansions** (Boston: Houghton Mifflin, 1925)

Clarke, Eliot C., **MAIN DRAINAGE WORKS OF THE CITY OF BOSTON, 2nd edition** (Boston: Rockwell & Churchill, 1885)

Coleman, Charles L., **HISTORY OF THE NEGRO BAPTISTS IN BOSTON** (unpublished Master's Thesis, Andover-Newton Theological School, 1956)

Daniels, John, **IN FREEDOM'S BIRTHPLACE: A Study of Boston Negroes** (Boston: Houghton Mifflin, 1914)

Edward, Kheable M., **THE NEGRO IN BOSTON** (Boston: Action For Boston Community Development, 1961)

Essex Institute, **DIARY OF WILLIAM BENTLEY, D.D., Pastor of East Church in Salem** (Salem: The Essex Institute, 1905)

Frazier, Thomas R., editor, **AFRO-AMERICAN HISTORY: PRIMARY SOURCES, Prince Hall's "A Charge Delivered to the Brethren of the African Lodge, June 24, 1797 at Menotomy"** (New York: Harcourt Brace Jovanoich, 1970)

Gardner, John S., Rector of Trinity Church, "**A Sermon Preached Before the African Society on the 14th of July 1810, The Anniversary of the Abolition of the Slave Trade.**" (Boston: Munroe & Francis, Printers, 1810) — Collections of the American Antiquarian Society

Grady, Anne, "**African Americans in Boston 1790-1820**" (draft of a report for the Society for the Preservation of New England Antiquities, 1995)

Handlin, Oscar, **BOSTON'S IMMAGRANTS** (Cambridge: Harvard University Press, 1979)

Hayden, Robert C., **AFRICAN AMERICANS IN BOSTON: More than 350 Years** (Boston: Trustees of the Public Library of Boston, 1991)

_____, **THE AFRICAN MEETING HOUSE IN BOSTON** (Boston: Museum of Afro-American History, 1987)

Horton, James Oliver and Lois E. Horton, **BLACK BOSTONIANS: Family Life and Community Struggle in the Antebellum North** (New York: Holmes & Meier, 1999)

Johnston, Johanna, **PAUL CUFFEE: America's First Black Captain** (New York: Dodd Mead, 1970)

Kirker, Harold and James Kirker, **BULLFINCH'S BOSTON: 1787-1817** (New York: Oxford University Press, 1964)

Kirsch, George, **BIOGRAPHY OF JEREMY BELKNAP** (Manchester, New Hampshire: Ayer Company Publishers, 1982)

Levesque, George A., **BLACK BOSTON: African American Life and Culture in Urban America 1750-1860** (New York: Garland Publishing Company, 1994)

McKillop, Joan, **"Amazing Grace"** (on-line article from The Cowper and Newton Bulletin, Vol. 2, No. 1, 2003)

Morse, Jedidiah, D.D., Pastor of the Congregational Church, Charlestown, **"A Discourse Delivered at the African meeting house in Boston, July 14, 1808 in Celebration of the Abolition of the Slave Trade."** (Boston: Lincoln & Edmands Printers, 1808) – Collections of the American Antiquarian Society

Nell, William C., **COLORED PATRIOTS OF THE AMERICAN REVOLUTION** (Boston: 1855, reprint by Arno Press, New York, 1968)

Parsons, William S. and Margaret A. Drew, **THE AFRICAN MEETING HOUSE IN BOSTON: A Sourcebook** (Boston: Museum of Afro-American History, 1988)

Quincy, Josiah, **MUNICIPAL HISTORY OF THE TOWN AND CITY OF BOSTON** (Boston: Charles Little & James Brown, 1852)

Seasholes, Nancy S., **GAINING GROUND: A History of Land-Making in Boston** (Cambridge: Massachusetts Institute of Technology Press, 2003)

Shurtleff, Nathaniel B., **TOPOGRAPHICAL AND HISTORICAL DESCRIPTION OF BOSTON** (Boston: Rockwell & Churchill, 1890)

Spear, Chloe, **MEMOIR OF CHLOE SPEAR: A Native of Africa Who Was Enslaved in Childhood** (Boston: James Loring, 1832)

Rosebrock, Ellen Fletcher, **"A Historical Account of the Joy Street Block Between Myrtle and Cambridge Streets,"** Report prepared for the Museum of Afro-American History, Dec. 22, 1978)

Thwing, Annie H., **CROOKED AND NARROW STREETS OF BOSTON** (Boston: Marshall Jones Company, 1920)

White, Shane, **"It Was a Proud Day: African Americans' Festivals and**

Parades in the North 1741-1834 (Journal of American History, 81, June 1994, pp. 13-50)

Whitehill, Walter M., **BOSTON: A Topographical History** (Cambridge: Harvard University Press, 1959)

Some additional sources:

Bennett, Lerone, Jr., **THE SHAPING OF BLACK AMERICA** (New York: Penguin Books, 1993)

Davis, David Brion, **CHALLENGING THE BOUNDARIES OF SLAVERY** (Cambridge: Harvard University Press, 2003)

Horton, James Oliver, and Lois E. Horton, **SLAVERY AND THE MAKING OF AMERICA** (Oxford and New York: Oxford University Press, 2005)

Levine, Lawrence W., **BLACK CULTURE AND BLACK CONSCIOUSNESS: Afro-American Folk Thought From Slavery to Freedom** (Oxford and New York: Oxford University Press, 1978)

Primary Source, Inc., **A SONG FULL OF HOPE, 1770-1830**, Source Book Two in the curriculum series, MAKING FREEDOM: African Americans in U.S. History (Portsmouth: Heinemann, 2004)

ABOUT THE AUTHOR: After more than thirty years working, writing and volunteering on behalf of New England's early history, Patricia Quigley Wall has become a serious student of the region's early African American history. Her first historical novel on that topic, CHILD OUT OF PLACE: A Story of New England (Fall Rose Books, 2004) awakened the interest of thousands of 4th and 5th graders and their teachers. And, unexpectedly, it found an enthusiastic readership among adults throughout this region and well beyond. Mrs. Wall grew up in Germantown, Pennsylvania and now lives in Kittery Point, Maine.